Cabel

Cabel

PAUL K. McAFEE

A Black Horse Western

ROBERT HALE · LONDON

To Shirley, my love

ISBN 0 7090 6164 1

Robert Hale Limited
Clerkenwell House
Clerkenwell Green
London EC1R 0HT

Photoset in North Wales by
Derek Doyle & Associates, Mold, Flintshire.
Printed and bound in Great Britain by
WBC Book Manufacturers Limited,
Bridgend.

One

He leaned against the bar in one of Smithville's three saloons. Lean and spare, slightly over six feet tall, his eyes a gray-green Scottish gleam in the dim light of the room, he searched the faces of three men playing a slow game of stud poker at a table at the end of the bar.

The bartender came up the bar, wiping a spot of spilled beer. Tossing his damp rag aside he eyed the newest customer in the room.

'What'll you have, friend?' he said, his tones indicating he cared little about what the customer bought, just that he bought something.

'A beer,' said the man. His denim jacket stretched thinly across his broad shoulders, over a worn blue shirt. Pants faded blue, thrust into scuffed boots, bore a dim yellow strip down the side. Held there by a cartridge belt with shells gleaming dully, a .44 Colt rested on his right hip. Slung low in a well-used holster, with thong over the hammer, the butt of the revolver showed the effects of care. It was a land just finished with the throes of a bloody war, and violence was part of life, as much as breathing or eating. Most men, and some women, carried firearms, and many were very adept with their usage. On the other hand, the weapons were carried for protection against animals and varmints of savage or poisonous nature.

The bartender served the beer and picked up the coin laid on the counter by the man. Stranger to the bartender, there was no conversation between the two. The barkeep moved on down the varnished length of wood, and began working with some glasses and placing them on a shelf back of him, eyeing the stranger in the long mirror there.

One of the men at the table had been watching the man at the bar. He pushed back his hat and laid aside his hand. 'I fold. Deal me out of the next hand,' he told his companions. He rose from his chair and moved toward the center of the room.

'You at the bar,' he called loudly. 'Turn around so's I kin get a good look at you.' He stood straddle-legged, his right hand resting on his gunbelt close to his weapon.

The stranger turned slowly and looked at him, unspeaking.

'Quiet one, ain't you,' remarked the man facing him. 'What's your moniker? Cain't say I've ever seen you hereabouts. I'm Arley Hawkins, an' I'm the quickest gun in these parts.'

There came no answer. The gray-green eyes scanned Arley Hawkins, seeing the tied-down handgun on Hawkins's right hip, the curled fingers a few inches from the gun butt. The eyes took in the unshaven face, the quirky smile and the eyes that seemed to move constantly, taking in the room and all present. Finally he spoke.

'My name is Josh Cabel,' he said, the voice cool and quiet. His right hand dropped and thumbed the thong off the hammer of his sixgun. As he spoke his name the barkeep stopped what he was doing and looked intently at the man.

'Cabel, huh?' responded Hawkins. 'I guess I've heered that name a time or two. But I seen you loosen up yore gun. Reckon you can take me?'

'I want no trouble with you,' Cabel said. 'I came in for a drink and some information.'

'You've had yore drink. Now's the time for you to face off with me. I'm buildin' me a rep as a gunnie,' said Hawkins, a sly grin on his lips. 'Now, you either draw or raise yore hands an' walk out that door, like a whipped pup.'

Cabel shook his head. 'I have no quarrel with you, Hawkins. I never saw you before in my life. Just drop it and we'll go on with whatever we were doing.'

Hawkins shook his head. 'Nope. You may be a notch on my gun or be knowed as a coward because you was afeerd of me. Now draw or walk – it's yore choice.'

The barkeep spoke up. 'Arley, you're drunk. Now get out an' sleep it off. Don't start something that'll just bring trouble for everyone . . . .'

'Shut up, Ben!' yelled Hawkins. 'I'll 'tend to you later. Now . . . .' he glared at Cabel and his right hand swept down toward his gun butt.

He's fast, thought Cabel, and he is mean. As the thought raced through his mind, his gun leaped from its leather and roared! Smoke belched between them and Hawkins screamed and looked down at his right hand. The gun was still in his holster, but two of his fingers were no longer on his hand. He clutched his fist and screamed again.

'You've ruined me!' he yelled. 'I ain't got no

fingers left on my hand, damn you!'

Coolly Cabel thrust the spent shell from the chamber of his sixgun and pushed another load in its place. He looked at Hawkins, his face still and unexpressive.

'You can either forget about being a gunnie,' he said, 'or learn to use your gun lefthanded. Now, you have a choice.' With one last look at the groaning gunman, he turned back to the barkeep.

'Is Orval Brock still sheriff here in Smithville?'

'He shore is, Cabel,' said the barkeep, Ben Turpin, 'an' he's jist comin' through th' door.'

TWO

Orval Brock had been sheriff of this and other towns for over twenty years. He was known to be one with courage and ability to head off trouble or take care of it when it appeared. He strode through the batwing doors of the saloon casually, keen, cool eyes sweeping the scene. Three men around a card table, one cuddling a bleeding hand. One man leaning against the bar watching him as he entered, and Ben Turpin, the barkeep, back of the bar, leaning on the polished wood, with a serious face.

'What's goin' on, Ben?' the sheriff asked, pausing a few feet from the wounded man and eyeing him carefully. He nodded to Arley Hawkins. 'What's wrong with Arley?'

'That stranger there just up an' shot my hand off!' Arley said, before Ben could answer the sheriff. Brock glanced at Ben and the bartender shook his head.

'That's not the way of it, Orval,' Ben said. He nodded toward Hawkins. 'Arley there decided to start his rep as a gunnie and started on the wrong man.'

The sheriff looked keenly at Cabel. 'I think I

11

should know you,' he said. 'Do you mind tellin' me who you are?'

'I'm Josh Cabel, Sheriff. I grew up in this town. I've been busy for the past four years.'

Brock nodded, a wry smile touching his lips beneath his ample mustache. 'I reckon you have. I thought I recognized you. Si Cabel's boy, huh? Went off to the war.'

Cabel nodded, without answering. Arley Hawkins yelled at the sheriff, 'Orval, you gonna palaver with that gunnie there, or put him ahind bars for shootin' a innocent man?'

Again Ben Turpin intervened. 'Here's how it was, Orval.' In a few terse sentences he filled the sheriff in on the happening. When he finished Brock sighed and shook his head.

'Arley, if I had fifty dollars for every time I've had to jail you, I'd be rich an' retired, instead of a tired old sheriff. I'll send a deputy along and when the doctor gets him patched up, bring him to the jail. I'll be waitin', so don't try to slip outta town.' He turned to Josh Cabel.

'It's nice to see a few of you gettin' back with whole hides, Josh. Come on down to the jail. I happen to have a favorite bottle there, that Ben, here, don't know about. Better'n anything he's ever served across his bar.' The mustache stirred in a slight grin.

Josh eased away from the bar, watching as Hawkins's two friends led him from the bar and down the street. 'Much obliged, Orval,' he said. 'I've got a few questions for you.'

In his office, Brock gestured for Josh to take a hardbacked chair near the desk, while he reached into a drawer and brought out a bottle and two glasses. He wiped the glasses with a towel and poured into each an inch of the whiskey.

'Good Kentucky bourbon.' He raised the glass to Josh. 'Here's to your good health and luck in gettin' through a war with a whole skin.' They both tossed off the whiskey and the sheriff poured again, then seated himself behind the desk.

'I reckon you want to know about your folks,' he mused. He shook his head. 'You want to talk to Doc Henry after I fill you in. He took care of them.'

'What actually happened, Orval?' asked Josh, his face tight, his eyes narrowed.

The sheriff was silent for a long moment then sighed and shook his head. 'It should never have happened, Josh. You know about Bill Quantrill and his gang sackin' an' burnin' Laurenceville, an' killin' a whole lot of innocent folks. That was in August '63. Well, after they had razed that town, they split up for they knowed the army and the law, what there was of it, would be after them. Six of them split off from the main gang and come through Smithville.' He fell silent, brooding.

'They started in whoopin' an' shootin' into houses. Yore pa run out to see what was goin' on, an' one of them shot him down and then another took time to empty a gun into your ma and your sister when they come runnin' to see what was happening. All three of them dead.'

Josh Cabel sat chilled. He had been informed that his parents were dead but none of the circumstances surrounding their deaths had reached him. His sister was barely sixteen years old, just finished the local grade school that spring, graduating with honors from the eighth grade and thinking of taking examinations to become a teacher.

Anger coursed through him. Shot down like animals in the street . . . killed by dregs of humanity who attached themselves to a killer like Quantrill for the pleasure of marauding, killing and stealing under the guise of the Confederacy, which never recognized or supported Quantrill nor his gang. Murderers of his people. His anger shook him and he sat shivering under the eyes of the old sheriff.

'Much obliged, Orval. I know you done what you could.'

Brock nodded. 'I got there in time to kill one of them and wound another. But five of them got away.'

'Did you know the name of any of the five?' asked Cabel, his voice cold and level. His eyes bored into those of the lawman.

Brock shook his head. 'Talk to Doc Henry, Josh. He'll fill in the rest any of us knows about them.'

Josh nodded and left the office.

Standing on the boardwalk outside the office, Josh rolled a Bull Durham and scratched a sulfur match against the doorframe. Drawing in a lungful of pungent smoke, he let it trickle out of his mouth and nose slowly, savoring the taste and effect of the tobacco. Doctor Amos Henry's office was down the street a few yards from the sheriff's office, over the only mercantile store in Smithville. Josh shook his shoulders and stepped away from the building. Might as well get it over with, he thought. But he dreaded the full knowledge of the murder of his parents and sister.

Josh stood before three graves in the cemetery back of Smithville's Methodist Church. He had gone, reluctantly, boy-like, to Sunday School classes in the old church. He had sat beside his parents and sister during long, (to him) dull sermons given by the same, now elderly, minister standing beside him, looking down at the graves. Reverend Thomas Francis Cartwright, distant relative to a circuit-riding Cartwright of the midwest some years back.

'There was some money at the house, those raiders missed,' the minister murmured to him. 'I used it to give your ma and pa and sister a good funeral and burial.' He looked up into the still, set face of the young man. 'Don't become bitter, Josh. Remember your mother's Christianity and try to gather from it some forgiveness and understanding . . . .'

'Reverend,' Josh's voice was tight with his grief and his no little anger, 'forgiveness and understanding are words I don't understand right now. Revenge is more likely to come to mind.'

'Oh, Josh . . . .'

'Reverend,' Josh faced the kindly old minister, whose face now mirrored his concern for the young man before him. 'My parents and little sister lie here dead. Made dead by some rabid gunman who then ravished my home and stole articles, money and horses belonging to my father – to me. That calls for some accounting on the part of the criminals.' His voice seethed with hate and fury. 'I intend to get a full accounting!'

'You may run afoul of the law if you are not careful of your actions,' warned the old man, his hands shaking as he touched the arm of the young man before him. 'That would do neither you nor your dead parents and sister any good.'

'Within the law, or outside of the law, Reverend, I intend to face the murderers and settle my account and my parents' with them.' His face softened. 'Thank you, sir, for what you did for them. I shall never forget it. From time to time you will hear from me. And one day, perhaps, we will stand here together again and I will be in a better frame of mind.'

The old minister nodded, his face pained as they turned away and walked back to the front of the church where Josh's horse awaited him. 'Pray God it will be so,' he said softly. They shook hands and mounting his horse, Josh left. The minister's face was sad as he watched the tall, young man guide his horse out of Smithville.

Josh made camp beside a small creek some miles from Smithville. Over a fire, he roasted a rabbit he killed along the trail. The plump young animal done, he brought out a can of tomatoes and some biscuits the preacher's wife had given him after he had lunched with them before visiting the cemetery.

The fresh meat, the taste of the tomatoes and the bread formed a pleasant meal for the young man. He relaxed near the small fire, leaning back against his saddle. Near by his hobbled horse made comfortable noises grazing. He recalled his conversation with the Smithville sheriff.

'Where did you learn to shoot like that?' Brock had asked. 'Or was that just a fluke?'

Josh shook his head. 'No, I meant to shoot the gun out of his hand as he drew. But he was slow and I took his hand instead.' He shook his head. 'He would never have made it as a shootist.'

'Where'd you learn to shoot like that?'

Josh looked at the sheriff. 'Ever hear of Sam Bass?'

The sheriff nodded.

'Bass was in my company at Shiloh and after for a little while,' Josh said. 'He taught me to draw reasonably fast and then take the time to aim. Most fast-draw shootists miss their first shot, high or off to the side, or into the ground in front of their opponent. It's their second shot that counts. Bass taught me to draw, fast enough and smooth and then aim and fire before your opponent gets off his second shot. I learned to do that pretty good.'

'Sam Bass was with Quantrill when he raided Lawrenceville in August '63,' said the sheriff. 'He wasn't in the army then.'

'Bass just walked away from the army one night,' Josh said. 'He said army fighting was too tame for him. He wanted more fighting, not walking for miles, and then fighting for a few hours and then long waits. He just up and left. I never knew he had joined up with Quantrill.' Josh asked the sheriff a question. 'Who was it that raided Smithville and killed my parents and sister?'

The sheriff was silent a moment and then stirred. He reached into a desk drawer and taking out a scrap of paper he wrote a name on it. 'I never knew the entire five,' he said, 'but I knew who the leader was. Here's his name.' He handed the scrap of paper to Josh. 'The last I heard, he was settled down somewhere near Denver, back in the canyon country. Had a ranch there.'

Sitting by the fire, comfortable and nibbling on a final rabbit leg, Josh reached into his shirt pocket

and pulled out the scrap of paper. The name of John
Baker was printed there in bold letters. Baker had
led the small gang into Smithville, which was only
five miles along their escape route. There they shot
up the town some, raced down the street where
Josh's parents lived. Seeing the Cabels run from their
house to see what the disturbance might be, he had
opened fire upon them. Others of his gang did the
same. With a wild yell, Baker had waved them on,
seeing the three Cabels dead and dying.

Sheriff Orval Brock had appeared on the scene
belatedly. But his keen rifle shot had knocked Ike
Hall from his saddle, who died as he hit the ground,
the bullet bursting his heart.

Josh looked at the name on the paper, seen dimly
in the light of the fire. John Baker, he thought.
According to the sheriff he was one of Quantrill's
lieutenants. He was ruthless, a gunman of known
ability, and never hesitant to use it. Josh sighed. Men
change names as well as places. John Baker could
very well be Henry Goodfellow and a well-regarded
citizen in some community. But the sheriff had said
Denver and the canyon country. If Baker was there,
with a ranch, then it was possible some of the other
members of his gang would be close by.

He replaced the paper in his shirt pocket and
leaned forward to add some wood to the fire. Bushes
crackled back of him and he whirled, his hand flashing to his sixgun at his side.

In a blur of motion he saw two figures burst into
the small clearing where he had camped, causing his
horse to snort and bound awkwardly out of their way.
One held a rifle, pointing in his direction. The other
was lifting a sixgun from his holster.

'You crippled our buddy, Arley, this morning,' one yelled, his hat flying from his head in his rush toward Josh. 'Now we mean to do you in! No one shoots a friend of ours for no good reason and gets away with it!'

Three

Josh rolled from the saddle where he had been lean-ing, drawing his sixgun as he rolled, ending up across the fire from the two charging men. As he ceased rolling he thrust his gun forward, earing back the hammer and squeezing off a quick shot. His aim was accurate.

The one with the rifle skidded to a halt at the edge of the fire and yelling in pain dropped the long gun and grabbed his stomach. His eyes blared and he staggered back and sat down hard.

The small clearing roared with gunfire as the one with the sixgun raced around the fire, shooting at Josh with every step. Quickly, Josh rolled again, keep-ing the fire between him and his enemy, and fired across the flames. The smoke and the movement of the man caused him to miss. He ducked as a bullet creased his shoulder and another kicked up dirt in his face. Then the looming form of the man was before him, paused and aiming down and leering. 'Gottya,' he growled. 'Looks like you've sent my pardner on his last go 'round. But now it's yore turn.'

Just at that moment Josh's horse snorted and stamped in irritation at the scent of gunsmoke wafting over him, and the roar of the guns. His snort and trampling in the bushes startled the man with the gun and he, unthinking, turned his head. He realized too late what he had done, and cursing jerked off a shot at Josh. But the second of inattention cost him his life. Josh's sixgun hammered a second before the other, and a small, blue hole appeared in the man's forehead. Josh fired again, emptying his sixgun, his final bullet drilling the man dead center in the chest. The man dropped the gun, and fell to the ground, landing hard and rolling. He twitched, heaved one last breath and was dead.

Quickly Josh pushed the empties from the chambers of his gun and, plucking fresh loads from his belt, refilled the weapon. He lay quietly where he was, listening. A small wind rustled the leaves of the trees about the clearing. His horse, no longer frightened by the gunsmoke and noise, returned to grazing.

Apparently the two men had decided to square their friend Arley's account with Josh Cabel without further help. Josh rose from the ground, brushing off dirt and grimacing at a twisted muscle in his back. He approached both bodies cautiously, his gun ready. Playing 'possum was an old trick. But this was no game. Both were dead.

Kneeling beside the body Josh searched the man for some identification. In a worn wallet he found a few dollars, and a scrap of paper with an address of someone in Ohio. He placed the paper and wallet back in a shirt pocket.

His search of the other turned up no information as to the name or address to which information might be mailed. He rose and dusted off his knees.

Arley Hawkins might be able to give the sheriff their names, he thought. And the bodies would be buried in one corner of Smithville Methodist Church cemetery, set aside there for just such purpose, the burial of 'John Does'.

The visitors' horses had been left two hundred yards away, ground-haltered. Josh found them easily and bringing them to the clearing, unsaddled them. Each of the bodies he rolled in a blanket and tarp. Tomorrow he would take them back to Smithville and turn them over to Sheriff Brock, with the explanation of what happened. He sighed. He had experienced, in a few short months, more violence than most men received in a lifetime. The war years, the blood-letting of the battlefields, Shiloh, Chickamauga, Sherman's drive through Georgia – now it seemed to be following him. And he was seeking more, as he followed the trail of those who had murdered his parents and sister.

He doused the fire and, rolled in his blankets and tarp back in the shadows of the trees surrounding the clearing, he spent long hours of the night attempting to picture what the future might hold for him.

Sheriff Orval Brock stepped from his office as Josh drew up to the rail across the boardwalk from him.

Brock eyed the bundled bodies on the horses and then slanted a steely glance at Josh.

'You draw trouble like molasses draw flies, don't you?' he said. Josh slid from the saddle and threw the reins over the rail. He nodded at the two bodies.

'They came looking for me last night, after dark. Thought I was asleep or dozing, and rushed me. I heard them in time and, well . . . you see the results.'

'Who are they?' Brock asked, standing beside one of the bodies. 'Ever seen them before?'

Josh nodded. 'They were the friends of Arley Hawkins. They come at me to get even for my wounding Hawkins. Or so one of them yelled as he came at me.'

The sheriff grunted, sighed and then shrugged. 'Guess you did what anyone would do under the same circumstances, defend himself.' He called in the office door, 'Jake, get these two heroes down to the Doc's place. Then take Arley down there and have him identify them.' He raised his eyebrows at Josh. 'Did you find any identification on them?'

Josh shook his head. 'Nope. There's an address on a piece of paper in one of their pockets. There's nothing on the other one to tell who he was.'

The deputy came out of the office and, taking the reins of the horses, he walked off down the street to deliver the dead men to the doctor, who served as the town's undertaker.

'Come down to the bar,' Brock said. 'You can fill me in more and then I have a suggestion for you.'

Josh strolled with him down the boardwalk, their spurs dragging and chiming back of them. Brock was neat from his early morning shave, having done nothing to become disheveled. Josh was dusty from his ride in from the plains and the dusty roads back into Smithville. As they entered the relative cool darkness of the saloon, he removed his hat and dusted it against his leg.

Ben Turpin, the bartender, recognized Josh immediately and nodded. 'Beers?' he asked. The sheriff and Josh took a table close to the outside wall. The

sheriff noticed that Josh took the chair with his back
to the wall, facing the door.

'Don't think anything's gonna happen this early in
the day,' he said dryly to Josh. Turpin brought the
beers over with a dish of corn kernels roasted in
bacon fat.

'Stayin' long this time?' he asked Josh.

'He ain't,' Brock answered for Josh. 'He's got business over Denver way, ain't that right, Josh?'

Josh nodded. 'Thanks for the beer, Orval.' He
nodded to Ben. 'Yes, I'm leaving as soon as I can turn
my hoss toward Denver,' he said, raising the bottle to
his mouth and taking a long swallow.

Ben turned to go and then, rather hesitantly,
turned back. 'Josh, I knowed your dad for a long
time. I remember you as a kid runnin' around here.
You went away to war and now are back.' He looked
quizzically at Josh. 'Are you really a shootist?'

Josh looked at the barkeep, sipping his beer at the
same time. He shook his head. 'Nope, Ben, like a lot
of men during the war, I learned a lot about guns. It
seems I had a natural flair for the rifle and for the
sidearm. I was given some instruction by one that
knew much more than anyone else about how to
handle the sixgun. He had one with him.' He
shrugged. 'I had a lot of occasions to use that talent.
Maybe that's why I'm here, talking to you now. But,
no, I am not a shootist, a gunnie, or whatever you call
them. I just happen to be pretty good with the
sidearm, and there's very few who can slip up on me
without my knowing it.'

Ben looked at Josh a long time and then nodded.
'I believe you, boy, but not everyone will. There'll be
some looking you up, just to see for themselves just

how good you really are.' He returned to the bar and busied himself wiping the already highly polished top.

The sheriff sat his emptied bottle on the table and leaned back in the chair. 'My suggestion I mentioned is just that you vacate these premises now. Get on your way to Colorado. Forget about Arley Hawkins and his ilk. I'll take care of seein' about them two you sent on their way last night. It was purely self defense, in my book. An' I'll record it that way.'

Josh swallowed the last of his beer and sat the bottle beside the sheriff's empty one. He pulled his hat down firmly in place and rose, the chair scraping on the floor as he did so.

'Good suggestion, Orval. I'll be on my way right now. And I do thank you for seeing my side of the shooting.'

As Josh and the sheriff stepped out of the saloon, Jake walked past them, hazing Arley Hawkins toward the jail. At the sight of Josh, Hawkins slid to a stop and thrust his bandaged hand at Josh. He cursed Josh viciously. Josh simply looked at him and made no reply.

'I'll be seein' you, Cabel. I'll get even for what you did to me, and for murdering my two buddies.'

'There was no murder, Arley,' Sheriff Brock told him coldly. 'Jake, get this scum back behind bars.' When they were out of earshot, he faced Josh.

'I can't really hold him long, Josh. Just a couple of days an' I'll have to let him go. You be a long ways from here by then and you'll have no trouble with Arley.' He thrust out his hand, grasping Josh's in a firm grip.

'Good luck, Josh. I hear tell Denver is right purty,

even if it is a mile high and colder than the north pole in winter. If you get through here again, look me up. I'll be here.'

When Josh rode out of town, he glanced back to see that the sheriff stood before his office. The officer waved his hat at him, and then entered the building. Josh gigged his horse and in a few minutes left the small town, where he had lived out his early years, behind him. Ahead of him was a trail of revenge. Somewhere, somehow, the killers of his parents and sister would get their just reward . . . death by the son and brother of those innocent people they had slaughtered.

Josh sat his horse at the edge of a wide mesa. Back of him reared the craggy teeth of the Rocky Mountains, the higher ones holding snow, glistening in the late evening sun. Before him spread the plains reaching south and west toward Mexico and further ranges of mountains showed a blue-purple presence.

On the edge of the mesa directly below him a figure darted out of a tumble of huge rocks. Josh's keen eyes noted a thin trail disappearing among them. The figure dashed along the trail, looking back over his shoulder, straining, black hair streaming behind him. His clothing seemed a brown or tan, much like those made of animal hides. An Indian? thought Josh.

Josh was startled by sudden reports, gunshots, coming from the jumble of rocks A figure raced his horse from the shadows of the rocks, reined it in, and leaping from the saddle, knelt in the dust, aiming a rifle at the running figure.

A second man appeared on top of the nearest

rock, also bearing a rifle. He, too, aimed at the darting figure on the trail before them.

The rifle of the kneeling man fired, smoke spurting from the barrel, the sound of the report coming up the grade to where Josh sat his horse. The man on the rock also fired, quickly ejected the spent shell and fired again.

The running man staggered, lurched forward a few strides and then sprawled, twisting in trail. A yell came from one of the men doing the shooting, and both aimed at the prone body again.

Josh did not like the odds. The running man was apparently unarmed. Two against one, both armed and one not, did not seem right. It was none of his business, but Josh did not like the odds against the man, now wounded or perhaps dead. Without hesitation he drew his rifle from the saddle sheath and fired into the air. The sound of the shot rolled down the slope of the mesa, and the two men jerked about, seeking the source.

Josh leaped to the ground and moving away from his mount, he knelt beside a pine and with a well-placed shot dusted the legs of the kneeling man. Moving his rifle slightly, Josh fired at the man standing on the rock. The round glanced off the granite at his feet, and whined away into the distance.

The kneeling man leaped to his horse, and the man on the rock disappeared. In a few moments they were gone, the sound of hoofs echoing above the rocks and a slight roll of dust tracing their passage away from the area.

Mounting, Josh worked his horse slowly and carefully down the slope of the land, until he was on the trail where the shooting had taken place. He rode up to the still figure lying in the trail, sprawled limply, showing no life.

Dismounting, Josh approached the body. Kneeling, he rolled it over onto its back. 'An Indian, by George,' Josh muttered. Blood covered the chest, flowing freely from a wound in the shoulder. There was also blood on one of the legs. Josh knelt there and sighed.

The Indian was young and alive, but seriously wounded. He could probably stop the bleeding, but proper care had to be found. Colorado City was a few miles away at the further edge of the mesa. But something had to be done right now, if the man was to live.

Josh lifted the Indian as carefully as possible and carried him to a shaded area of a pine. There he removed the man's shirt and winced when he saw the hole in the shoulder. An inch or two lower and it would have taken part of the lung and gone right into the heart.

Lifting the body he looked for an exit wound and found none. A purpling lump showed at the edge of the clavicle. He shrugged. The bullet had lodged just beneath the skin and would have to be cut out. As gently as possible he padded the front wound and bound it with strips torn from the shirt.

He then turned to the leg. With his bowie knife he slit the pant leg and saw that the bullet had passed through the meaty part of the left thigh and had apparently missed the large artery there. The blood was not spurting, but was pouring freely. He quickly used up the remainder of the shirt padding and binding the leg, putting a tourniquet above the wound. With the pressure of the pad, he would be able to remove the tourniquet in a short time.

Now, he thought, that's done. What am I going to do with him? He stood, stretching the kinks out of his back, looking about. His eyes caught the dark smudge of an overhanging ledge or even a small cave a few hundred yards up the slope across the trail from where he had entered.

Bringing his horse close, he lifted the inert body of the Indian and laid him across the saddle. Holding the man in place, he guided the animal and its burden up the slope, about huge boulders, threading through thickets and brush, until at last, winded and sweating, he eased the horse to a stop before the opening in the slope which Josh had seen from the trail.

Breathing deeply and wiping his face on his kerchief, he gave greater attention to the area. He was pleased to see that it was indeed a shallow cave, reaching back the length and width of a reasonable room of a house. The ceiling was low, and showed the effects of smoke blackening. It had been used as a refuge many times in the past.

Grunting with the effort, he eased the man from the saddle and into the cave. There he laid him down and saw that he was still deeply unconscious.

Within a few minutes Josh had his bedroll inside, the horse tethered nearby. He would find a place for the animal later. He spread out the blankets on a tarp which was part of his sleeping gear. Once prepared, he placed the Indian on the blankets.

Easing back against the wall of the cave, Josh took a sack of Bull Durham from a shirt pocket and rolled a cigarette. Pulling the smoke into his lungs, letting it escape through lips and nose, he assessed his situation.

A stranger in the area, he had observed an attempted murder. Now he had a wounded Indian to care for. The killers might return to find him and make certain he would not identify them. He drew on the cigarette and looked at the Indian.

'I don't know what's behind all this,' he mused, 'but I shore am in a predicament I didn't figure on.'

Four

Sam Crawford was a burly man nearing sixty years. He was about five ten, and weighing more than his frame called for. His nature was brusque which, along with constantly narrowed, cold blue eyes, light of color and slightly bulging, meant he was not one to be approached easily.

Crawford came into the Colorado canyon country while the Civil War was still being fought. There he bought out an elderly, sick rancher whose spread was the entirety of a wide, long valley. It was landlocked at one end, butting against a huge mesa, lifting into the Rocky Mountains. It spread six miles wide in places and was fifteen miles long, filled with wide meadows, rich grazing and enough timber to build several towns.

To this Sam Crawford brought his wife and one daughter. The wife died when the daughter was twelve years old, and Sam had raised her, with an Indian woman as a housekeeper. Here had been her home, with the exception of the long winter months, which she had spent with an elderly aunt in Cheyenne, Wyoming, at a school developed there for children of the area's population, such as himself. From April to October she lived in the valley, and became expert in horsemanship, managing cattle, and from time to time simply riding and exploring among an ancient Indian Pueblo village, now long abandoned, lifting tier upon tier upon a huge cliff at one side of the valley.

Sam named her after his mother who had died when he was a young man, Saralou. He doted upon her, spoiled her and gave in to most of her wishes. Now at eighteen years, Saralou Crawford was a pretty young woman, fulsome in stature, determined of mind and used to getting her own way. All those working upon the ranch loved her and had catered to her every wish since she had come into the valley.

Today she sat a young, spirited bay filly, just broken to ride by the wranglers at the ranch, and given her as a birthday present by her father. She put the young mare through her paces and was thinking of taking her out for a run along the small river that ran through the valley, when she noticed two men come racing into the yard before the house. They tossed reins over the hitch rail there, and dusting their hats against their legs, strode across the porch and knocked at the front door.

She knew them as members of the crew that ran the ranch under the rather harsh hand of her father. Ned Walker and Tim Rush. Both were fairly new to the outfit and she had not learned much about them. She did know her father had sent them out on a rather hurried trip two days ago. She watched as the Mexican housekeeper opened the door and let the two men into the house.

Sam Crawford eyed the two men before him. They were dusty from their ride and obviously anxious to get to the bunkhouse to stretch out for some rest. From Crawford's attitude, they knew their relaxation would be detained until the rancher was satisfied with their report.

'Did you find the Indian?' he asked Ned Walker. Both men nodded and Walker answered.

'Yeah, we found him all right. He was workin' his way toward the mountains, to get out of the valley.'

Crawford was silent a long moment, eyeing each man. Finally he nodded.

'All right, did you do what I told you to do? That Indian had to be made into a good Indian. And you know what General Sheridan said about that.'

Tim Rush grinned. 'A good Injun is a dead Injun . . . right, huh?'

'That's what he said and that was what I meant.' He leaned back in his chair, the slats creaking with his weight. 'Well?'

Ned Walker answered. 'Yeah, he's a good Injun, all right, Sam. We made shore of that.' Tim Rush nodded in agreement.

There was a long minute as the rancher eyed each and turned over in his mind what they had said. Finally he nodded.

'Very well,' he said. 'Now we get some grub from the cook and wash up a bit. Don't talk to anyone else about this. It is between you and me.' His face was grim. 'Understood?'

The two men stirred as to leave the room when the rancher stopped them. 'What did you do with the body?' he asked abruptly. 'We don't want it found and questions asked.'

'Uh, oh, we dragged him up the slope from the trail an' found an undercut bank in a wash,' Ned

Walker said hurriedly. 'We poked him in there and tumbled the ledge down over him an' then put some rocks over it to make it look natural-like.' Tim Rush nodded vigorously in agreement.

Sam Crawford studied the men. How far could he trust them? he thought. Did they really find and kill the Indian and then bury him, as they said? Yet, he had to take their word at face value. Otherwise, he would never be certain in his mind that the Indian would not appear again. He finally nodded slowly.

'All right. Go on and get cleaned up, and not one word to anyone about this, or you and me will be nose to nose.' He stared coldly at them and they both nodded and almost bolted from the room.

Crawford was restless. That Indian had been around the ranch since he was a youngun. He had been tolerated, kidded, abused now and then, but more or less accepted. Coins were given him for little jobs, when he was small. Then suddenly he was grown and an expert horseman, expert at training them, as many Indians were. Then he had to put his nose where it should not have been.

Crawford shook his head. It was a task for one man, he mused, to keep a large ranch operating, and have secrets that could not be shared. He started as his daughter appeared in the doorway of his office. He smiled and relaxed at the sight of her, the jewel of his life. She was of bright complexion, as had been her mother. Her eyes were dark green with moving lights that seemed to brighten every room she entered. At five feet six, she was no small girl, but well proportioned, with slim waist and fulsome bosom. In his eyes she was the most beautiful thing on earth.

'Hi, Daddy,' her voice was bright and firm. Her

lips, red with nature's gift, spread in a happy smile, over firm, white teeth. She approached the desk he sat behind, and sitting on one corner, she smiled down at him, swinging one booted foot.

'Hi, Sugar,' he peered up at her from under bushy eyebrows that were beginning to show a few strands of gray. 'What brings you in so early? I thought you would be trying out that new birthday present.'

'Oh, I did. She's wonderful, Daddy. Who trained her, Running Fox? He certainly has a gift with horses.'

He nodded, his face settling into sunburned and tanned folds. 'Yes. The Indian trained him. He told me the mare was the best he had ever worked with.'

'Well, he did a good job with her. When I see him, I'll tell him so.'

Crawford did not answer his daughter's last remark. Instead he turned the conversation another direction. 'There's a dance in Denver at the Masonic Hall come Saturday next. I suppose some dewy-eyed swain has asked you to go with him.'

Her eyes twinkled at him. 'I'll tell you later, Daddy. Now and then you don't like my escort and somehow get the message to him not to show up. Then I am escorted by my father.' She made a mouth at him.

'Can't blame me for wanting to show off the prettiest girl in Colorado, can you?'

She laughed at him and coming around the desk planted a kiss upon his upturned cheek. 'You are an old faker, you know that? Yes, I will be going to the dance and this time you will be pleased with my escort. You'll see.' She patted his cheek and left the room, turning to smile at him as she went through the door.

Sam Crawford sighed. He hoped to God this beautiful and innocent young daughter never learned of the mess he had gotten drawn into. He would try his best to keep it from her knowledge.

The Indian groaned and tossed on the blankets. Josh saw the sweat on the man's forehead and wiped it off with a rag. He had built a small fire at one side of the cave. He knew it was not the fire, but fever, that heated the Indian's body.

A small pool of water had collected in a natural basin just outside the ledge. Josh was somewhat concerned about food running low, for he carried only enough hard-tack and jerky for a few days. But the water close by was a godsend.

The Indian's wounds were red and puffy, but there seemed to be no infection forming. It was two nights now. He had not as yet regained full consciousness. Josh wondered how he would react when he saw he was being cared for by a white man.

The Indian groaned again and when Josh looked at him the black eyes opened. Puzzlement moved through them for a moment and then realization. With a snarl, the young Indian tried to sit, but fell back as the pain of his shoulder and leg engulfed him. He lay there, breathing deeply, glaring at Josh.

'Take it easy, *amigo*,' Josh said softly. 'You're safe here, at least for a while.' He hesitated and eyed the young Indian. 'Do you *comprendo Ingles?*' Josh thought to himself, I certainly hope so. I've used up just about all the Spanish I know. And who says he knows Spanish!

The Indian continued to glare at him and then

turned his head, his face reflecting his pain, and ignored Josh.

Josh shrugged. 'I guess not. Well, for whatever you can get out of this, you're shot in the shoulder, bad wound, and in the left leg, not bad. You've lost a lot of blood. You've been here one day and two nights. No one has come looking for you. So I guess I'll just have to load you on my hoss and tote you into Colorado City.'

The blackhaired head turned slowly on the pillow Josh had fashioned from a spare mackinaw he carried with his blankets. The black eyes opened and stared at him. The fever-dried lips stirred, the tongue came out and licked them and the throat moved.

'I speak English,' the voice whispered hoarsely. 'Much better than your Spanish.' The eyes closed and opened again. 'Do not take me to Colorado City. With your help, I can make my village and the medicine man can do what else needs doing for me.' He frowned and looked at Josh. 'Why are you doing all this for me? You can get yourself into much trouble giving me help and shelter.'

Josh shrugged. 'Whatever,' he said and smiled wryly. 'I saw two men chasing you and both shooting at you. You were unarmed, and I thought that was a little one-sided, so I loosed a couple of rounds to let them know someone else was around and they took off like scared jackrabbits.'

The young Indian eyed him silently. 'You *are* in trouble. This land belongs to a man called Crawford. He claims a valley rich with grass and woodlands, and some sacred grave sites of my people. He keeps all Indians away and I happen to be in the wrong place at the wrong time.'

Josh sensed there was more to the story. 'But why shoot to kill you? Would he have done the same with a white trespasser?'

The Indian was silent again. 'My people have lived in pueblos in the valley for centuries. He, Crawford, is trying to run us away from our homes. There are only a few of us left and we wish to remain on our land.'

Josh shook his head. 'Seems unfair, and a little unreal. But,' he grinned slightly, 'now that we can talk, I'm Josh Cabel. I'm out here looking for someone. But the question now is, how can I get you to your village, when this Crawford don't want you to cross his land?'

A stolid look settled upon the Indian's face. 'I am called Robert Running Fox. The mission school in Denver gave me the English name. I know ancient trails made long ago by the Old Ones. Very few know of them, they are few and hard to find and follow. My grandfather taught me to find them.'

'The Old Ones?' Josh rose and going to the edge of the cave looked out over the valley.

'Ancient forefathers,' explained Running Fox. 'They were called the Anasazi. They were here long ago,' he moved a hand to indicate space and time. 'Even before my grandfather's grandfather. Much time ago. They built the pueblo and my people have lived that way until recently.'

There suddenly was a rattle of stones outside the caves, and the sound of voices. Josh lowered himself and crept to the edge of the ledge and looked down . . . into the face of Ned Walker!

Five

Les Parker was foreman of the Bar-C Ranch. He had come into the valley with Crawford. He had spent years helping to build the ranch, knowing every inch and every coulée, every trail and every horse and how many beefs on the range.

Being foreman and trusted implicitly by Crawford, he did most of the hiring and firing of hands. Some had been with the ranch a long time, others were drifters, coming and going with the seasons. Such he deemed Ned Walker and Tim Rush to be. Not knowing them well, and none too pleased with their work, he was displeased when Crawford sent them out on a mission of which he, Parker, had not been informed. This irked him and he watched the two men very closely the next day or two.

Walker and Rush were down back of the corrals where the young horses were broken for work and ride. Lee Parker saw them there, their heads close together.

'We'd better set out there and really bury that Injun,' said Walker. 'Someone just might come along an' find him an' then we'd be up the creek with Crawford.'

'Well, he's dead, all right,' said Tim. 'But I guess

39

we oughta get him out of sight.' He looked at the sky. 'It's about chow time anyways. Let's grab a bite to eat an' then go do it.'

The two of them left the ranch as though going out to check some cattle. The foreman watched them thoughtfully. He was uneasy about them, didn't really know them. And Crawford had them doing something. He decided he would let it ride for a day or two and then if something like that occurred again, he would question Sam Crawford about it. After all, he was the range boss, the foreman, and the work of the ranch actually was his prerogative. He watched them out of sight and then turned his attention to a wrangler working out a new stallion in the horse corral.

The Indian's body was gone!

Walker and Rush found traces of blood where he had fallen after they shot him, but there was no body. Tim Rush immediately became agitated. He eyed the bushes about the trail where the Indian had fallen.

'We'd better scout around a little, Ned,' he said nervously. 'He just might be alive and hidin' out in them rocks over there.' He pointed to a jumble of boulders.

'Well, we hit 'em all right. There's blood.' Ned dismounted and walked around the spot. 'Here's hoofprints and . . . boot tracks. Someone's found him!'

Ned looked thoughtfully at the trail. He followed the hoofprints until they disappeared into the brush. Raising his eyes, he saw a dark ledge, several yards above the boulders Tim had mentioned. A cave, he thought, or a washed out ledge. Big enough to hide a couple of men. He called to Tim.

'I think he's up there under that ledge. Whoever found the Injun took him up there and pushed him in, I'll bet, an' left him there.'

Tim looked where he pointed. He nodded. 'Let's go look.' he said. Ground hitching their horses, they followed the hoofprints into the brush. Here and there the boot tracks appeared.

'He's holdin' the body of the dead Injun on his saddle,' Ned opined. 'Guess he's afraid of bein' caught with the dead Injun on his hands. Probably in trouble an' ridin' the lonesome trails.'

Just below the ledge Tim stumbled and slid on some rocks, several of them rattling down the slope. Ned froze where he was, and then lifted himself to look into the area under the ledge, and came face to face with Josh Cabel!

He ducked back and slipping behind a boulder, yelled at Tim, 'Look out! There's a feller up there an' he'll know why we are nosin' around. We gotta get him an' bury that Injun!'

'Bury 'em both together,' growled Tim. He drew his sixgun and, earing it back, blasted three quick rounds into the cave.

Josh rolled back away from the edge of the cave, drawing his sixgun as he did so. Running Fox rolled over, oblivious to his pains and grabbed Josh's rifle. They eyed each other and nodded and waited silently for what would happen next.

Ned decided to rush the cave opening, firing as he went, while Tim fired into the cave to keep whoever was inside busy to save his hide. With sixgun in hand Ned took a deep breath, then, yelling at the top of his voice, he rushed up the incline and ducking under the lip of the ledge began firing haphazardly into the cave.

As the lanky body of Ned Walker filled the cave opening, his sixgun bellowing and lead bouncing and screaming off the rock walls, Josh lay flat on the floor and, with heart pounding in his chest, fired at the intruder. His second bullet took Walker down and yelling, he fell off the ledge of the cave entrance and rolled into Tim Rush, who was settled to fire his rifle into the cave. His body took Tim's feet from under him, and both men rolled against a boulder and lay scratched and bleeding, half conscious and tangled together.

Tim got his senses straightened out and began to attempt to work his way out from under the groaning body of his partner. He finally pulled free and sat up to look into the black maw of Josh Cabel's sixgun.

'Just take it easy, friend,' said Josh quietly. 'Put your hands on your head and don't even think of that rifle laying over there. Now, how about your partner? Is he hurt bad?'

Tim glared at Josh and then nudged Ned. 'Ned, how bad are you hurt?'

Ned groaned. 'Oh, Gawd, don't shake me like that. I'm dyin'. He shot my legs to pieces.'

'I shot twice and hit you. You fell out of the cave,' Josh said.

Josh forced Tim to lie down and with the man's bandanna, tied his hands behind him. 'Now you lie there, unless you want a slug in you somewhere more serious than your partner.' Josh turned his attention to Ned.

Apparently one of Josh's bullets had shattered Ned's right knee. Cutting the man's pants away from the wound, Josh wrapped Ned's bandanna about the

wound, which was bleeding heavily, but not danger-
ously. Using Tim's belt, he placed a tourniquet above
the knee. Then, he forced Ned to lie down beside
Tim and stood looking down at them.

'I'm getting my rope and gonna hogtie you
together. If either of you tries to run, I'll use your
own rifle to cut you down.' He picked up the rifle.
'Now lie there and contemplate your sins.'

Neither man was inclined to test Josh's ability with
the rifle. In a few minutes they were tied together
and lay cursing each other, each blaming the other
for the predicament they were in.

Josh entered the cave, fearing Robert Running
Fox had been wounded again. But he found the
Indian awake and alert, the rifle lying beside him.

He looked quizzically at Josh as the cowboy
entered and then squatted down beside him. The
Indian eyed Josh silently. Josh shrugged.

'I shot one in the leg and have both of them tied
up. I found their horses. Both wear the Bar-C brand.'

Running Fox nodded. 'It figures,' he said. 'Sam
Crawford would have to make sure. He wouldn't take
no one's word. They had to come back to take some
proof to him that I was dead.'

Josh looked at him a long minute. 'Robert, there
is an extra horse, now. If I wrapped up your leg and
put your shoulder in some sort of a sling, do you
think you could use those old trails and get back to
your village, without being seen?'

The Indian nodded, his face grim. 'I can do,' he
grunted.

Josh rode into the yard of the big house. Bar-C was
burned on a plank nailed over the road leading in

from the range. As he rode up Les Parker came out of the main house and stood on the porch.

Josh eyed him, and then guided his mount to the hitch rail before the porch. He hooked a leg over his saddle horn and pointed a thumb back at Ned Walker and Tim Rush, trussed and bound, on a led horse, and riding double. Each began cursing and squirming as their mount came to a halt.

'These two belong here?' asked Josh calmly. He pulled his sack of Bull Durham from his shirt and quietly rolled a cigarette. His eyes never left the face of the foreman. He swept a match across the top of the saddle horn and lit the cigarette, drawing in smoke and letting it out, face calm and unconcerned.

Parker nodded shortly. 'I hate to admit it, but they do work here. What's this all mean?'

'He jumped us from the bushes,' yelled Tim. 'Shot Ned in the leg and then pushed me over a boulder with his hoss . . . .'

Parker glared at Tim. 'Shut your mouth, Rush!' He turned his eyes to Josh. 'You tell me what happened?'

'Yes, why don't you tell us why you have two of my hands tied up and one of them obviously wounded?'

Josh raised his eyes from the face of Parker and looked at Sam Crawford, who stepped from the doorway and stood beside the foreman. He was somewhat surprised to see a lithe, pretty young woman follow Crawford from the house and stand, leaning against the doorjamb, her eyes on his face and then upon the two bound men.

'Maybe I should ask who you might be?' asked Josh. 'I need to talk to the owner of the ranch and whoever pays the wages of these two varmints.'

Sam's face flushed with a quick anger. He was unused to being addressed so bluntly, especially while standing on his own front porch. 'I'm Sam Crawford. I own this spread,' he grunted.

'You all stand here gabbin',' gritted Ned Walker, 'an' I'm bleedin' to death. Get me down and at least do something about this knee.'

Crawford paused in whatever he was about to say and spoke to the foreman. 'Get them into the bunkhouse and see what the knee looks like. If it's real bad, put him in a buckboard and take him into town to a doctor.'

Parker stepped from the porch and taking the lead from Josh's hand, led the horse and its riders toward the bunkhouse. Crawford looked at Josh, his face grim. 'Now tell me what this is all about.'

Josh looked at him thoughtfully and nodded. In a quiet voice he explained his presence on the Bar-C, looking for work. Seeing an Indian shot he had taken the Indian into his camp in a cave nearby the main trail and bound up his wounds. The man remained unconscious for a day and a night before he stirred. But he seemed to come out of it all right.

Saralou stepped up beside her father. 'Did the Indian give you a name?'

Josh observed her for the first time. He smiled slightly and touched the brim of his hat. 'Yes, ma'am. By the way, my name is Joshua Cabel. The Indian said he was called Running Fox, Robert Running Fox.'

The girl's face paled. 'Oh, Daddy. Running Fox is hurt bad. Maybe dead.' She looked up at Josh. 'Did you leave him in the cave?'

Josh shook his head. 'No, ma'am. After those two

men attacked my camp and shot at us, I managed to take them prisoner, as you see. Running Fox said if I could bind him up better, and get him on one of the Bar-C hosses, he could make it to his village.'

Crawford's face tightened. It paled with anger and frustration. But he simply nodded at Josh's story. The girl relaxed obviously, and smiled at Josh.

'If Robert Running Fox said he could do something, he will do it,' she said. 'I'm Saralou Crawford,' she put an arm about Crawford's waist, 'and this is my father.' Her face became serious. 'Thank you for helping Running Fox. I can't figure out why anyone would want to shoot him, but there's a lot of white people who think any Indian is fair game.'

'I'm new in the country here,' said Josh. 'But I reckon you don't need hands, if you have men who just ride around hunting down Indians.' He picked up his reins. 'I'd be obliged, however, if I might water my hoss before I leave.'

Sam Crawford's mind was moving fast. What did this stranger know? Did he see Walker and Rush try to kill the Indian? And what had actually become of the Indian? He gestured and grimaced.

'Water your hoss and . . . .'

'Dad,' Saralou interrupted. 'Walker won't be able to work for several weeks, if his knee is as bad as it seems, even if you don't fire him. Which, by the way, I think you should. Robert Running Fox was a good man. Anyway, why not hire this man here – Mr Cabel – to do Walker's work, until you get to the bottom of all this?' She looked at her father and then at Josh, her face inscrutable.

Crawford's face flushed again. He had thought of this briefly, but this man was a stranger, and he had undoubtedly talked with Running Fox. However, he grunted and nodded.

'All right. But you keep away from Walker and his pal Rush. In fact, I have some critters over against the mesa that needs checking. You can work that range for me, until we get this all straightened out.' He turned to enter the house, when the foreman, Les Parker, came up from the bunkhouse.

'Walker's knee is in a bad shape, Sam,' he said. 'I'm going to send him into Colorado City to the doc there.'

Sam considered this and then nodded. 'All right. In the meantime, Cabel here will take Walker's place. Put him to work on the range out by the mesa.' He looked at Cabel. 'Pack up enough food to last you two weeks. I don't want to see you around here before that.'

The foreman frowned. Then he shrugged. 'Right, boss. I'll see him outfitted and on his way at daylight.' He motioned for Josh to follow him.

Josh glanced back over his shoulder at the girl. She stood in the doorway of the house. As he looked she smiled and then entered the room, closing the door back of her.

It is the far range, indeed, Josh thought as he guided his roan stallion up a steep grade and paused before a shack whose roof needed fixing and that leaned tiredly toward a huge pine beside it. Looks like a good wind would blow it over, he mused.

'Oh well,' he spoke to the roan. 'We take what we can get. We'll spend the summer here and then if I don't find what I'm looking for, we'll go somewhere else.' Noting a corral back of the cabin, he guided the horse there, and unsaddling it, slapped its flank and sent it into the grassy area. He closed the pole gate back of it and turned to the cabin.

It had not been used for some time. Packrats had built nests in corners, and birds had taken over the rafter joints for nesting. When he shoved the door open, there was a scampering of paws, squeaking of startled varmints and the squawk and rush of winged creatures.

He shugged. Clean it up, it was a place to sleep for the time he would be here. He brought in his personal gear, the food he had brought and blankets for the bunk. Going outside, he made certain the horse would be safe in the corral, the pole fence secure. A rickety shed next to the corral held some hay, cut and dried early in the season, piled in one corner. With a rusted pitchfork he tossed some of it to where the horse could reach it. This done he straightened and looked about him.

The cabin and corral were placed against a cliff, a towering hundred feet of red rock and slate. Facing away from it he looked into a distance which showed meadows, copses of aspen and scrub pines dotting them. The plain reached across the mesa, until the range ended at the rolling lift of a mountain range. One towering peak raised rough shoulders above the range, and Josh recalled someone telling him about Zebulon Pike, a mountain explorer, who discovered this peak. It was named after its discoverer, Pikes Peak. One day, thought Josh, I'll climb it, to see how far I can see.

Josh was satisfied. Colorado City was not far. He could enquire there about a man called John Baker. During his wandering Josh had learned that Baker had settled somewhere near Colorado City, back in canyon country. Someone would surely know of him. Unless he'd changed his name.

Josh shook his head. Time was not an enemy. It was a friend. Somewhere, somehow, Baker and he would come face to face, even if he had changed his name.

Riding the range for a week, Josh found cattle marked with Crawford's Bar-C brand on their hips. The herd had not moved far away from the lush meadows. Here and there a rangy young bull would snort and eye the horse and man. Not challenging him, but letting the intruder of his domain know he was seen. Keeping a wary eye out for such creatures, Josh covered the range in two or three days. There were calves to be branded at the fall roundup. Here and there was a maverick. These inspected carefully for no other brands, Josh would rope and brand before the fall gather started.

At the end of his first week on the job, Josh came from the cabin one morning and stopped short. Someone had been to the cabin that night during his sleep.

Hanging from a limb of a live oak in front of the cabin was the carcass of a young deer. It had been dressed out, and wrapped in hide; cached in the crotch of the limb were the heart and liver.

Someone had brought him fresh meat for his provisions. Josh smiled. He could not prove who had so favored him, but he had an idea of who it might have been.

Six

It was the middle of the second week. Josh was coming in from the range, having spent the day chasing mavericks, hogtieing them and burning the Bar-C brand upon their hips. He saw a rider crossing the small creek that ran in front of his cabin.

Les Parker drew up before the corral as Josh dismounted and opened the gate to the enclosure. The foreman sat looking down at Josh, whose outfit showed the effects of steer-wrestling and brush bursting chases.

'It looks like you's been busy all right,' Parker said. He eased in the saddle, pushing his hat back, eyeing Josh carefully.

'Plenty to do here,' Josh answered. He gestured to the cabin. 'Get down and come in. I'll stir up some grub for us.'

'Don't mind if I do,' said Parker. He dismounted and along with Josh, turned his horse into the corral. The horses cared for, Josh led the way into the cabin.

Parker viewed the inside. 'Not much of a place,' he said with a small grin. 'But, for your needs, I guess it's all right.'

Josh shrugged. 'Keeps the wind off me and the

rain out, but it don't rain much right now. It'll do, until winter.'

Les Parker drew up a chair to the table and watched as Josh washed and then began to put together a meal of potatoes, onions, venison and greens. Once it was all on the small iron stove, he sat down across the table from the foreman.

'What brings you out this far?' he asked, passing his sack of Bull Durham across to the foreman. Parker nodded his thanks and with his own paper, rolled a cigarette and lit it with a sulfur match. He shook out the match and tossed the wooden stem in a woodbox beside the stove.

'I noticed you're cookin' venison,' he said, not answering Josh's question. 'Got one, huh?'

Josh shook his head. 'Nope. It was a gift from someone. Found it hangin' from the tree out front the other morning.'

'Huh, that's strange. You made any friends out this way?' asked Parker.

Again Josh shook his head. 'Not a soul has come by to say howdy. Saw a rider cross the lower end of the mesa a week ago just after I got here. But, no one but my mysterious deermeat provider has been about. And there were no signs coming or going around the cabin.'

'Crawford wanted me to tell you to keep an eye out for that Injun you helped get away,' Harper said abruptly. 'He's suspicious about some thievin' that's been goin' on about the ranches hereabouts. If you see him, he wants you to bring him in so he can question him.'

Josh busied himself dishing up food. He sat down again across from the foreman and after a mouthful or two of food, replied to Parker.

'I didn't just help him get away, I bound up his wounds, and put him on one of the Bar-C hosses. He turned that hoss loose and it's grazing on one of the meadows. And I can't see shooting a man down, so Crawford could talk to him, like Walker and Rush did, is very friendly like. It's more like "a good Injun is a dead Injun".'

Parker shook his head, chewing on his food. He swallowed and pointed a fork at Josh. 'Ain't none of that any of yore business, Cabel. Sam Crawford had trusted that Injun boy an' give him a good job, wranglin' the fresh hosses to workable animals. Then he turned against the boss and run away, after making a move toward Miss Saralou.'

Josh ceased chewing and stared at the foreman. 'Miss Saralou argued for him with her father,' he said. He eyed the foreman narrowly. 'There's more to it than that.'

'Maybe,' agreed Parker, shrugging. 'But whatever it is, I'm just quotin' the boss, the man who will pay your wages end of this month. He wants you to come on in to headquarters so's he can talk to you about it. He wants to meet that Robert Running Fox face to face.'

Josh nodded and dropped the subject. 'Stay the night,' he suggested to the foreman. 'I'll ride in with you come morning.'

The following morning Josh and Parker left the cabin, and headed for the ranch headquarters. At the creek, as they allowed their mounts to drink before the day-long trip, Josh looked back at the cabin. His eyes lifted to the bluff above and back of the small structure. Red boulders, dark slate and gray-white slabs of rock reached up and up, with a few pines scattered across the surface. An eagle soared high above the cliff, drifting upon the uplifting currents. He saw nothing atop the cliff, no movement of animal or man. His horse finished drinking, he pulled its head up and gigged it with blunted spurs, urging it across the creek.

Shrouded by the shadow of a boulder, standing in a sharp crevice between the rock and the face of the cliff, Robert Running Fox watched the two riders out of sight. Waiting a further half-hour, to make certain neither of them returned to the cabin, he picked his way down the cliff, hidden by shadows and boulders until he stood at the back of the cabin.

There he stood and looked with vision-keen eyes and listened with ears tuned for any alien sounds. Seeing and hearing nothing other than the sounds of the earth about him, he quickly entered the cabin. He carried an article in his hands which he left on the bunk, covered with the top blanket. Pausing in the doorway he looked and listened again and then left as quickly and as silently as he had come.

'Ned Walker is back at the ranch,' Parker told Josh. 'He's doin' odd jobs until his knee gets completely healed. Just ignore him but don't be surprised if he tries to take you on.'

'After what he did to the Indian, Crawford intends to keep him on?' asked Josh, surprise written on his face.

Parker nodded shortly. 'It's the boss's call. I'd send him packin', along with Rush, if it was my doin'. But I'm jist the tophand and so-called foreman. The old man overrides my orders and suggestions purty regularly.'

It was late afternoon, nearing suppertime when the two arrived at the ranch. They both tended to their horses, and then went to the bunkhouse. There were several empty bunks and Parker pointed to one not being used.

'That'll be yours whenever you're back here. Wash up an' come on over to the messhall next door. Cookie will be ringin' the supper call any minute.' He paused at the door and looked back at Josh. 'Walker will be there and so will Rush. Try not to get into no fracas.'

Josh shrugged. He placed his roll of blankets and tarp on the bunk, along with his rifle, and went outside to the wash bench. Cook, and apparently roustabout, the man had placed a bucket of water, with coarse wash cloths and towels on the bench.

As he finished with his washing up, Josh heard the cook's triangle being hammered in front of the messhall. He walked over and entered the building. Rush, Walker, Parker and three other hands were already at long tables with well-worn eating utensils in front of them. As Josh entered, 'Cookie' came in with steaming bowls of food and placed them before the men.

Parker headed to a seat at the end of the bench on which he sat. Across the room, adjacent to Parker, was Walker and beside him, his sidekick, Tim Rush. As Josh sat down Walker looked over, surprise on his face. Then anger flushed his features and he pointed a shaking finger at Josh, as he directed his remark to the foreman.

'If that skunk there is goin' to eat in the same mess

with me, I'll walk out and take care of the stink when he comes out!'

'Set down and eat,' Parker said to him, iron in his voice. 'Cabel is a hand on this ranch, and right now he's doing more than twice what you do.'

'He got me this way!' snarled Walker. He lunged out of his seat. Slapping Tim Rush on the back, he yelled, 'Come on out, pardner! We'll both work on this varmint.' Tim took a final mouthful of food and pushed erect, and after a sheepish glance at the foreman, followed Walker from the room.

'They'll both be waitin' for you,' one of the hands told Josh. 'They're mean and dirty. I've seen 'em fight. Watch their feet.'

Josh nodded. 'Right now, I'm interested in this food. Reckon they can wait a little while.' The cowboy grinned at him and nudged the man sitting next to him.

'I've got me a feelin' that this is gonna be worth watchin'.'

Josh did not comment. He did not want to get into a fracas with Walker and Rush. But he was not one to back away from trouble. He continued and finished a last cup of coffee.

He rose from his seat and looked at the foreman. Parker had pushed back and was lighting a cigarette. Through the first smoke his eyes looked questioningly at Cabel.

'I didn't want no fight with them,' Cabel told him. 'But I ain't backing off from them. Unless you want the scrap, however it might end, you'll have to call it off.'

Parker drew on his smoke, letting it out slowly. He shrugged. 'Might as well get it over with, Cabel,' he

said. 'But I'll see that there's no gunplay.' He rose
and looked Josh over. 'You ain't carryin' no iron, so
I'll make sure they ain't either.' He walked out of the
messhall, Josh at his heels.

Walker and Rush were standing straddle-legged
ten feet from the doorway, Walker paused and glared
at them.

'I reckon this fight just had to be. I'm pretty sure I
know what happened out there at the cave where you
found Cabel and the Indian. But it's your story
against his.' Parker paused then continued.
'Howsomever, there won't be any gunplay. So shuck
your irons, boys, an' hand 'em to me.'

'Not me,' yelled Walker. 'He crippled me for life.
I'm gonna make shore he never gets a chance to do
it to anyone else – ever.'

Parker shook his head. 'Cabel ain't carryin',' he
said. 'You shoot an unarmed man, Walker, an' I'll see
you hung, myself.'

Rush quickly removed his gunbelt and handed it
to Parker. But Walker was not taking the foreman's
word for it. 'Get him out here where I can see for
myself whether he's got a gun.'

Josh stepped past Parker and faced Walker. 'See
for yourself. Now, I don't want to fight you. What's
past is past. But I won't be pushed.'

'Wa'al, I'm doin' the pushin',' Walker said and
stepping toward Josh, lashed out with a large, closed
fist. Josh ducked and felt a blow to his kidney area.
He whirled and saw Rush grinning at him and pois-
ing for another blow.

Cabel ducked another awkward blow from Walker
and ignoring him momentarily, seized Rush by the
forearm and threw him over his leg. Rush landed

hard on his face before the steps of the messhall.

By this time all of the men were out of the messhall and grouped about the battling trio. Walker was red in the face from effort and anger, and yelling, cursing, launched himself at Josh.

Backing away from Walker, Josh stepped to one side of Rush, and caught him about the shoulders. He thrust Walker back and lashed out with his first real blow of the fight, all of the weight of his husky body behind it. It caught Walker squarely upon his jaw in front of the ear, and the man fell, his eyes rolling up in his head. He was sprawled, dazed and confused by the one blow.

Josh whirled and looked at Rush who was coming at him. Suddenly there was a keen-bladed knife in Rush's hand. He held it low, blade up, the indication of a knowledgeable knife fighter.

'He's got a sticker, Cabel,' one of the men yelled.

Josh crouched, circling with his opponent. He had been in knife fights before. It was dangerous, and tricky. He had picked up a few moves of his own during his years in the army and otherwise. He watched the eyes of Rush. The unblinking eyes, squinted and watchful, were the mirrors of the man's intentions.

Suddenly Rush gestured toward Josh with his left arm, and thinking Cabel was watching the movement, thrust quickly with the knife toward Josh's belly. Josh turned and leaned back and as the knife arm came at him, he clubbed down with all his might, and the knife dropped from Rush's numbed hand.

Rush tried to catch himself from the headlong lunge, but met Josh's fist in his belly. He grunted and bent momentarily with the blow, but the moment was enough for Cabel. His knee slammed into Rush's face and jaw. He straightened, his nose and mouth bleeding. As he did so Josh struck two quick blows to the face, left to the nose and then right once again, devastatingly accurate to his opponent's jaw. Rush staggered back and, tripping over his own feet, fell and lay unconscious beside his still dazed partner.

Josh stepped back. Except for the blow to the kidney area, given by Rush from behind, he had not been touched. The men about him grinned and shook their heads.

'Remind me,' one said to another, 'not to get into any fights with that boy. He's got a right fist like a sledgehammer.'

'Knows his way about a fight, too,' the man replied. Parker stepped down through the circle of men. He eyed Josh critically and then a wry smile crossed his tight-lipped mouth.

Before he spoke, a voice growled from the direction of the main house. The men in the circle knew the voice and broke up, turning to look toward its source.

'What's goin' on?' asked Crawford, coming up. His quick eyes saw the prone body of Rush, and Walker just rising to a sitting position, holding his head and groaning.

Parker spoke up. 'Walker decided to get even with Cabel for the bad knee. Rush obliged by enterin' the fracas as added incentive.'

'Two on one, eh? Hardly fair.' He looked over the two men in the dirt. He sighed and shook his head. 'Sure is bad when two men cain't whip one.' His eyes searched Josh's face. 'You must be pretty good with yore fists.' He looked thoughtfully at Cabel and then down at the defeated men again, then spoke to Parker.

'Get them on their feet. Fire them. I want both off the place as soon as they can ride. You,' he motioned to Josh, 'come on up to the house. I want to talk with you.'

Seven

Hanibal Kane owned the largest and most popular saloon in Colorado City. He had won enough in poker games on a Mississippi River gambling boat to purchase the business from an elderly owner who was on his last legs.

He spent most of his time in the saloon at one of the back tables, watching over business at the bar and the tables about the room, where various games of chance were conducted. Some were playing against the house dealers; the others were pick-up games among the men of the town, or in off the ranches in the immediate territory.

When the stranger walked into the saloon and up to the bar, Kane looked him over carefully. Not a bank roll there, he mused. Looks like he's just off the trail, maybe being chased by some federal marshal. Maybe just riding through, but obviously not capable of dropping much silver or gold into Kane's coffers.

The stranger bought a drink and turned his back to the bar, looking over those already in the room.

Kane watched the stranger. He appeared to be in his middle twenties. Kane also noted a sixgun on his right hip, turned forward for the cross-draw, so the gun was fired with the left hand. The stranger wore gloves and kept his right hand low, rather unobservable.

The barkeep brought the drink and received the coin in payment. 'Stranger comin' through, eh?' he asked the newcomer, wiping the bar, and ready to strike up a conversation.

'Yup,' was the answer.

'Lookin' for work, I suspect, huh? There might be some around, roundup ain't fer away.'

The stranger eyed him. 'Maybe. I could use a job. But I need some information more.'

'Oh?' The barkeep knew he was on thin ice now. Hanibal Kane was in the room, watching, and he frowned upon the saloon crew, barkeep, roustabout or girls, getting into long conversations. There were always kegs of whiskey and beer to be logged in and other things to be done about the saloon. 'What kind of information?' he asked hesitantly.

The stranger spoke softly. 'Have you seen any stranger around recently? Especially any asking for a certain man?'

The barkeep started to move away slowly, polishing a glass as he moved. He shook his head. 'Nope, cain't say that I have. But what's the name he might be askin' about?'

'Has a feller by the name of Josh Cabel been in here, been in town, as you know of?' The man had not answered the barkeep's question. His voice was low and only the barkeep saw his lips move.

Apprehensive of the boss getting on him for carrying on such a long talk with the stranger, the barkeep merely shook his head.

The stranger spoke again, now answering the

barkeep's question. 'If a stranger comes in asking for a man named John Baker, let me know.' He passed over a five dollar gold piece to the barkeep. 'I'll be around town awhile, or maybe working on one of the roundups. I'll check back with you.'

Apparently Hanibal Kane had especially keen hearing and had heard the last part of the conversation clearly from the bar. He rose from the table and walked over to the bar. He motioned for the barkeep.

'Give me one of the usual, Charlie,' he ordered, 'and give this young man another of what he just had – on me.' The barkeep hurried to do his boss's bidding. Kane smiled at the young stranger.

'Looking for someone, eh?'

The man smiled and nodded. 'Is there a John Baker around, that you know of? Or a cowpoke by the name of Josh Cabel?'

Hanibal shook his head slowly, thoughtfully. 'No,' he said slowly. 'Can't say that I know of either one of them.' He thrust out his hand. 'I'm Hanibal Kane, I own this joint.'

The man met his hand, eyeing him carefully. 'My name is Arley Hawkins,' he said. 'I just wanted to see Cabel for something personal.'

Hearing the name of John Baker stirred Hanibal Kane's memory of the incident. He had thought all such names and relationships with certain individuals were quieted. Oh, certainly the name of Quantrill rose frequently. Papers and magazines and now some books, would not let the rape of Lawrenceville, Kansas, die; there were individuals and families with too close a knowledge of all that transpired during the slaughter and burning of an entire town for it to die out completely. He shook his head. The raid was

now past history. One day only historians would
think of it. He shrugged and again sat at his favorite
table, sipping at his whiskey, losing himself in the
pleasure of the moment.

Walker and Rush were fired the night of the fight
with Josh Cabel, and left early the following morning. Les Parker withstood all their haranguing, his
face impassive, but his eyes narrowed and lips
compressed in anger. He watched in silence as the
men saddled their personal mounts and prepared to
leave the ranch.

As their departure lifted dust into the air, Ned
Walker's voice shouted back above the hoofbeats.
'This spread ain't heard the last of me, not by a long
shot!'

Parker sighed, shrugged and walked to the
bunkhouse where he kept a small, barren office. A
desk, two chairs, a clutter of old magazines, a book or
two, bridles, leather straps, lassos and other items of
a horseman or busy range boss.

Josh Cabel ate his breakfast and busied himself
about the horse corrals, selecting certain animals
that Crawford had indicated might need inspecting
and treated for various ailments before the fall
roundup.

He thought of the talk he had had with Crawford
the previous evening. They had gone to Crawford's
office and the rancher had questions concerning the
cattle on the mesa range. He questioned Josh about
the horse, now free on the meadows of the mesa,
near the line shack.

'Are you certain it is the same animal that you gave
the Indian when he was wounded? He might have

run in some spavined Indian cayuse old as the hills
and blind as well.'

Josh assured him it was the horse he had put the
Indian on and seen ride away. He had roped the
animal and examined its brand as well as inspecting
it for any damage. The horse was as good as it was
when he had last seen it.

The questioning went on for an hour and finally
Crawford let him go with a last remark, strange to
Josh's thinking. 'Have you seen anyone around the
cliff house, the pueblos, along the mesa?' Josh
assured him he had not.

With that Josh had gone to the bunkhouse and his
blankets. Now as he worked over the horses all of this
ran through his mind.

'Good morning, Josh.' He turned from where he
leaned against the corral poles for a moment's rest,
inspecting the horse tied to the snubbing post in the
center of the corral. It looked fine, but he wanted to
make sure. As he leaned against the corral poles and
smoked, he had not heard anyone approach. He
turned to face Saralou Crawford, the rancher's
daughter. This was the first time he had seen her
close up. His eyes took in the rich, brunette hair,
brushed back and tied with a red ribbon. Her eyes, a
changing green, sparkled with life and she smiled as
she looked up at Josh, whose even six feet did not
loom over her greatly. She was a rather tall girl.

'Er – howdy, Miss Crawford,' he answered, somewhat belatedly, for his scrutiny of her had taken a few
seconds. His mind was still swirling with the sight of
her figure, a deep bosom with a slim waist encircled
with a belt woven of soft leather, and beaded with
Indian colors. He politely touched the brim of his hat.

'My name is Saralou, Josh, and everyone calls me by my name. I want to get better acquainted with you. You were here briefly and then put away out there on the mesa. I suspect it is lonely out there, isn't it?'

He nodded and dropping his smoke, ground it out in the dust of the corral. 'Yes, it is. There's no pretty girls like you around, you can bet. In fact, none at all.'

She blushed slightly at his compliment. She looked at him and came close and leaned upon the poles, outside the corral, looking up at him and smiling, showing even, white teeth, through rosy lips that caused Josh's heart to flipflop. 'Are you going to be around for a while now?' she asked.

Josh nodded. 'For a little while, I reckon. Your dad wants me to go over the remuda before the roundups.' He nodded toward the horse he had snubbed to the post in the corral. 'Like that one there.'

'That's good.' she said. 'By the way, there's a dance in Colorado City Saturday evening. Perhaps you would like to go to it. You need some fun and relaxation after those long days out on the mesa with only cows and your bronc to talk to.' She looked up at him, her eyes suddenly serious.

'Well, it's been a spell since I had a chance to go to a shindig,' he mused. 'I just might do that, if a certain boss's daughter saved me a dance. I know she must have a lot of cowpokes and others, who'd give a pretty penny to do just that.'

She dropped her head, blushing again. Then she looked up at him and nodded. 'You're on, Josh. And I'm sure you are a very good dancer.'

He shook his head and grinned. 'I have stepped

on plenty of toes in my time, but I'll do my best.'

With that she touched his arm gently, looked intently at him for a long moment and turning, walked back toward the main house, her lithe body swaying in the sun.

Josh Cabel's heart was not the only one pounding a bit faster than usual. As she considered what she had done, she was a bit surprised at herself; usually she was never so forward.

In a shed doorway, Les Parker watched the young people, and his face darkened and lips compressed into a thin line. He did not like what he had heard and seen. For some time now, he had waited to make his move toward Saralou. He decided immediately now was the time to make it.

Eight

The dance was held on a wooden platform built between the church and the mercantile store in Colorado City [now Colorado Springs]. It was held following the spring roundup, in July for midsummer relaxation. There was usually another dance following the fall roundup. People from all over the territory came into the town for those important occasions.

The platform was railed, with an opening upon the street. There the sheriff or his deputy had a table where they collected the weapons of the men going onto the dance floor. No weapons were allowed beyond the railing. The rule was strict and Mark Spears, the sheriff, saw that it was religiously adhered to.

'We're here for fun,' he said. 'And I'll coldcock the first one who breaks it and throw him in jail for a week. While he's there he'll sweep floors, empty night buckets and spittoons. So, boys, come on in and have fun, but leave your trouble makers at home or shuck them off and leave them with us.' This rule was, most generally, adhered to without question.

Josh rode into Colorado City with Les Parker and others from the ranch. Crawford and Saralou had left the day before for business and pleasure. His business, her pleasure in shopping at the few general stores, and especially the shop where ladies' hats and shawls were for sale.

When Josh and Parker rode up and hitched their horses at the rail provided for such, the fiddler and guitar player were tuning up. A portly gentleman with a goatee was fingering the strings of a slap-bass fiddle and another was tuning a banjo, preparing for the dances to come.

As the long twilight lingered, couples began to appear. Townspeople mingled with ranchers and cowboys, businessmen with farmers. There was a quiet hum of mingled conversations, growing as the crowd grew, filled with voices, tuning instruments, some raucous laughter, shouts of greetings and a general cacophony of sound.

'Do you want to visit the saloon for a little nip before you go after some pretty gal to dosi-do with?' Parker asked, as they loosened the girths on their mounts and put feedbags of corn and oats about their noses.

'Nope, not really,' Josh said. 'Maybe later.'

Parker grinned. 'In a hurry to take some pretty gal onto the dance floor, huh?'

Josh nodded gravely, his eyes twinkling. 'If I can find one brave enough to look at this ugly mug of mine and trust her toes won't be tramped on too much.'

Parker laughed. 'OK. You go on. I'll see you later.' He left Josh and walked, swaggeringly, up the board-walk to the nearest saloon.

Josh walked slowly toward the dance platform. It was encircled with both men and women. Men were approaching the sheriff's deputy behind the table, and handing over their weapons. At the top of the steps they paused and dropped a quarter in a box held by a pretty teenage girl. The money was to be used to purchase new books for the school.

As he approached the dance platform Cabel heard his name called and looked around.

'Here, Josh, up here.' He raised his head and saw Saralou Crawford leaning against the platform railing, smiling down at him.

'Come on up, slow-poke,' she called, 'the first dance is about to start.'

'You mean you saved the first dance for me?' he asked, removing his belt and weapon and handing it to the deputy.

'No, you're second. I'm going to dance with my father and then when the next set starts, you had better be up here and ready.'

'Look real fast, Saralou,' he laughed as he spoke, a quiet happiness filling him, 'I'm ready there.'

She waved at him and as the first set was called, moved off to meet her father on the dance floor. Josh mounted the steps, pausing to drop some coins in the box the girl held, and took his place against the rail, watching the dancers, listening to the music and tapping his foot to the rhythm. It occurred to him that this was the first time, since he had learned of his parents' death and how they died, that he had felt so at peace with himself.

The dancers on the floor finished the set with a flourish of swinging skirts and stamping feet, and the music ended in rising triumphant notes. There was applause and the raising again of voices, as the rail leaners sought out partners from the feminine onlookers for the next dance. Josh straightened from leaning against the rail as the joyful-faced Saralou came skipping through the crowd to face him.

'Come on, Josh,' she called, her face flushed with the physical efforts of dancing, and the excitement of the moment. 'This time, it's your turn.'

Josh grinned at her. 'Are you sure you want to subject your toes to my awkward feet?'

She held out a hand as the caller of the dance announced a waltz. 'I suspect I will find you the best man dancer on the floor,' she smiled at him and grasped his hand, leading him through the other dancers.

'Remember that when there's a sudden pain in your big toe,' Josh laughed. He followed her to the cleared space on the platform just as the musicians began playing the music, indeed a waltz.

She came into his arms, slightly shorter than himself, her face lifted and happy. Josh was not the best dancer on the floor, but he knew his way around the waltz. They swung to the music and chatted softly now and then.

When the set was over, it was time for the musicians to take a break. Josh escorted Saralou to where her father stood along the railing. As Josh thanked her for the dance, Crawford looked sharply at him.

'Enjoying yourself, Cabel?' he asked in his rough voice. The tone said that that was his daughter and that he was not especially elated to have a mere cowhand, one who was almost a stranger, holding her in his arms – even on a crowded dance floor.

'Yes,' Josh replied, his eyes calmly meeting those of

Crawford. 'This seems to be a nice party. Your daughter is a very good dancer.'

Crawford grunted and turned away. Saralou was gathered up by two girls her own age, and smiling a goodbye to Josh, she disappeared among the women gathered at the other side of the platform.

Josh was reasonably certain the one dance was all he would get with the girl. He still recalled her perfume, light and subtle, her smiling eyes and the lithe body, close to him, but not pressing, during the dance. His heart beat faster, his mind was filled with her candid beauty and the fact that she seemed to enjoy his company.

In the shadows of a small building fronting the dance platform, fifty feet or more from the dancers, Arley Hawkins stood, his face twisted in anger as he watched Josh Cabel dancing with the pretty girl. His heart pounded. He had found him! His fingerless right hand clenched as his anger soared. Now! Now, by all that was holy, he had Josh Cabel where he wanted him.

Hawkins turned to a huge hulking Roy French standing beside him. He had hooked up with the man while in Colorado City. French was a six-foot-five, 220-pound individual with a slow mind. Arley Hawkins had seen a way to use the man, and had allowed him to follow him around from time to time, giving him money for drinks. French was used by the townspeople for odd jobs, dirty jobs with which they did not wish to soil their hands. Hawkins had seen him as a source of strength, seeing that many of the citizens of the city feared him. Now, he would use him. He turned to the sweat-tinged form beside him, smelling the odors of unwashed body, stale with tobacco stink and whiskey.

'Now, Roy, here is what I want you to do.' He drew close to the man, his nose filled with the rude odors that clung to him, and whispered intently in his ear. Roy French nodded vigorously, jerking his head up and down in agreement.

Nine

Les Parker had a few beers at the saloon and decided it was time he went to the dance. He was not much for prancing around with other men's girls and wives. He was more of a railsitter, watching the dancing, listening to the music and making certain none of his hands got into serious trouble. There were bottles and jugs of 'white lightning' stashed away in some wagons or behind bushes near the dance floor. And there was a constant stream of visitors to the locations of such nectars from which to imbibe.

Parker knew Sheriff Mark Spears, whose office was in Colorado City. The jail adjoining the office of the sheriff was constantly the abode of those who became drunk and disorderly. He did not hesitate to hustle such an individual – cowboy, mountain man or townsman – behind the bars until he cooled down. Parker knew the sheriff well and did not want any of his hands, needed at the ranch, losing working time back of those bars.

He approached the dance platform just as the final set was being called. It was close to midnight and people had long trips home, some from so far it might be midday or early evening before they arrived. He saw several of his hands dancing and some leaning on the platform railing. He did not intend to dance. He leaned against a nearby wagon wheel and watched and listened.

Not far from him was a man, a gun hanging on the right side, butt forward. A cross-draw, he thought. What've we got here? A shootist in town? He watched as the man conversed intently with a huge townsman standing beside him. The big man was nodding in agreement to something.

The music finished with a flourish and began the traditional departure melody of 'Good Night, Ladies'. Couples swung into this short final dance, and as it ended, applauded the musicians and began leaving the platform.

Josh had not had the final dance with Saralou. In fact, she had danced with her father, it being a ritual between them that she gave him the first and last dance. Josh fell in with those leaving the platform, moving slowly, laughing and talking among themselves. As he reached the lower step of the platform, a huge form appeared out of the crowd and stood weaving before him. Josh did not know him, but recalled seeing him in a saloon several weeks ago when he asked some discreet questions about work in the area. Standing before him was a man who obviously was drinking, in fact was drunk.

'You, there,' the large blunt finger prodded Cabel in the chest. 'Ah've gotta bone to pick with you.'

Josh eyed him levelly. The man was drunk. He did not know the man, but he judged him to be over two hundred pounds, standing several inches taller than Josh. He looked into the ugly features and a thin sliver of excitement ran down his spin. That one was wanting to pick a fight. And Josh knew he was at a disadvantage before it started. Yet, he did not back away, but watched the man's eyes. So far as he could see, he was unarmed, seeing no sixgun. There might be a knife or a hideout pistol somewhere on the huge frame.

'I never danced with your girl. You've got the wrong man. Now, let me pass. We're holding up the parade here.'

The huge head shook no. 'Uh'uh,' he grunted. 'I'm gonna wipe up the ground with you. No one touches my gal but me.' He drew back a fist the size of a small ham, and slammed it at Josh's face.

Josh ducked under the arm, and turning quickly, backpeddled away from the man. 'What's your name?' he asked as the man turned and stepped toward him again. 'I don't want to fight someone I don't know.'

'I'm Roy French. Ever'one knows me in town. There ain't a feller in this county that kin whup me.'

'Then let's not fight. You don't need my notch on your victory pole.' Josh turned to walk away.

With a yell, French launched himself at Josh. Seeing the looks on some faces of those gathered about the two, Josh sidestepped quickly. As French stumbled by him, he threw a hard right fist into French's kidney, causing the man to yell in pain and frustration. As the big man slid to a stop and turned to meet Josh, he met an equally hard fist to the jaw, with Josh's weight back of it. Shoulders and arms strong from years of wrestling with reluctant cayuses and angered bulls, branding kicking mavericks and wrestling kicking, protesting steers for branding, had given him muscles and strength that belied his size.

Josh's fist met Roy's jaw and the big man's head snapped back. He pawed the air and Josh's left fist buried itself in the big man's belly. Whiskey-scented air belched from French's mouth and he backed up, gasping for his breath.

Knowing he had to finish the fight soon, or French's weight and height would wear him down, Josh moved in with quick blows to the face and belly. But French had gotten a second wind. His massive arms clasped about Josh and lifted him from the ground. Grunting with effort, French swung his opponent a full circle and let him go. Josh flew through the air and landed on his shoulders and back at the edge of the circle of onlookers.

Before he could move, French leaped at him and kicked wih a huge foot, catching him in the short-ribs and driving wind from him. Seizing Josh by an arm, French jerked him to his feet, and reared back, fist balled and poised to smash into the smaller man's face.

The fight had moved away from the dance platform, down the street and now the struggle was before the Red Dog Saloon where Les Parker had had his beers. The crowd stayed with the fight, yelling, encouraging first one and then the other. A few on the fringes of the fight bet as to whom they thought would be the winner.

Josh ducked French's well-telegraphed right fist, feeling it glaze his shoulder. It shook him but he forged in under the swing and hammered at the big man's belly. This was telling on French, for he backed away, grunting for breath and in pain. Josh sidestepped French's next lunge and sank another kidney punch. Out of breath, hurting, French staggered to the small stoop lifting off the boardwalk in front of the batwing doors of the saloon. He sank on the porch, leaning his massive head against an upright post.

Warily, Josh came over and sat down beside him, his chest heaving from the fight, his arms limp from the physical encounters with the big man. French lifted his head from the post and raised bleary eyes to Josh's face.

'Who won?' he muttered.

Josh whooshed out a deep breath. He shook his head. 'I'm not sure,' he said. 'But, Roy, you're the best I ever fought with.'

French nodded. 'I'm good, all right,' he said, admitting to his prowess in street fighting. 'But, fer a leetle feller, you shore kin put up a scrap.'

'Why don't we go in here, and have a beer – on me?' Josh suggested. French thought about it for a moment and then nodded. He struggled to his feet, wavering. Josh got up from the edge of the porch and stood beside him. He looked out at the crowd about them. 'It's over, so you might as well go home,' he said.

Standing back of the crowd before the saloon, Arley Hawkins ground his teeth in anger. He had slipped Roy French a five dollar gold piece to beat up on Josh Caleb. He had gloried in the fight and the power the big man had exercised, pressing the smaller Josh and pounding him with gigantic fists. But the smaller man was in shape, finely toned by hard work in the sun and winds of the high country on the mesa. He had not won the fight, but Roy French had lost interest in the scrap and now the two of them rose and went into the saloon together like lifetime friends.

Had French killed Cabel in the fist fight – and the power in his gigantic body could have done so – Hawkins would have been elated. In fact, when he saw them sitting on the porch together, and he realized his incitement had been thwarted, he half drew his sixgun and would have murdered Cabel right then. But there were many close enough to recognize him and report to the sheriff. He did not know that Les Parker was watching his every move, and that had he drawn and prepared to loose a round at Josh, he would have been gunned down by the Bar-C foreman.

In the saloon Josh led the way to a table to one side of the room. He called to the barkeep to bring each of them a beer and paid for it when it came. He sat and sipped the beer, house warm, and looked at French.

'Why did you pick on me for a fight, Roy?' he asked.

French looked at him, puzzled. 'Now that you mention it, I don't rightly remember.' He thought a moment and then shook his massive head. 'Someone give me a gold piece to fight you,' he said. 'I don't get many five dollar gold pieces, these days.'

Josh sipped his beer, aching here and there where the big fists of the man had connected. His eyes thoughtful on Roy French, he saw beneath the surface of drinking and near poverty, the man was basically honest. True, he seemed somewhat retarded, or was it due to continued drinking and the fact that he had lost regard for himself?

'Roy,' Josh said softly, 'how long has it been since you had a job that gave you a place to stay, food to eat and a little money at the end of the month?'

A wry grin crossed the big man's face. 'I can't remember,' he mumbled. 'Seems a long time ago that I had any money that someone didn't just hand me, or I got fer odd jobs here an' there.'

'Would you like to work on a ranch?' Josh asked, an idea forming.

The big head nodded affirmatively. 'Yeah, but who'd hire me? Ever'one looks on me as a drunk an' no good.'

Josh finished his beer. He eyed French gravely. 'You stop your drinking and get some sleep and a good breakfast. I'll see you tomorrow, and I might have a job for you.' He paused. 'Don't get your hopes too high, but I think I know where there's a job you can handle.' He handed French five dollars in silver. 'This is to help you get cleaned up and a good meal.'

French lumbered to his feet. 'I'll be sober and cleaned up when you see me tomorrow,' he said, his face twisted with a hint of emotion. 'I'll be ready.'

Les Parker stood on the stoop of the hotel and listened to Josh. He knew French as a drunk and roustabout. But to hire him on as a hand had not occurred to him.

'How do you know he'll work the cattle with you out there on the mesa?' he asked Josh. 'Ain't it a gamble? He might just keep on drinkin' an' you'll have a drunk on your hands as well as cattle to look after.'

Josh nodded. 'I ain't got a glass ball to look into and see the future,' he said. 'But I think there's good in the man. You need help for the roundup, with Walker and Rush gone. French will help me round up the mesa herd and work it into the valley for the roundup.'

Parker weighed the need of hands against the knowledge he had of French, which he admitted, was mostly momentary observation and hearsay. Finally he agreed.

'All right,' he said. 'But he's in your charge. If he don't work out, he'll be fired no matter what you say.'

Arley Hawkins sat in a squalid room back of a saloon in Colorado City and chortled to himself. He had seen a face in the crowd about the saloon at the end of the fight between Josh and the roustabout French. A face that brought about memories, and that gave him an up on Joshua Cabel. Wait until I spring it on him, he thought with a twisted amusement. Won't he be surprised! And mad! Then, I'll have him where I want him!

Ten

After a week of doing without his whiskey crutch, Roy French began to show his worth as a cowboy. His body was soft from months of drinking and lack of exercise. But slowly he firmed up and by the end of the third week was clear eyed, working without complaint. He became saddle-sore and then toughened to the long day in the saddle. Slowly he slimmed down and by the time the first month was gone, his eyes were clear, his movements quicker and more accurate, and his loyalty to Josh Cabel deep and lasting. The young cowboy had believed in him, seen him in a job that paid, and worked with him through the first painful weeks.

Les Parker rode out to the mesa one time to see how the two were progressing and was satisfied that the former roustabout was indeed recovering from his earlier state. He went so far as to agree, partially, with Josh that French was coming along and would make a good hand.

'Start bringing the cattle down in about six weeks,' he said. 'After that we'll drift them back here and you can get set for the winter.' He looked about. 'Seems this shack could do with some work before the snows come.'

When Josh and French first arrived at the cabin at the base of the mesa rise, they prepared a meal and, tired from the day-long trip from the ranch head-quarters, sought their bunks.

As Josh pulled back the covers of his bunk, he stood stock still looking down in surprise. Covered by the blanket was a long object, wrapped in deerskin. He turned to ask French about it, but the man had left the cabin to make sure the horses were safe in the corral.

Josh took the long object and slowly unwrapped the deerskin, which was soft and pliant, prepared with much care, and stared at a rifle, new and obviously unused. Traces of the heavy grease in which such weapons came from the factory, were still on the piece.

Examining it closer Josh saw that the rifle was a Henry Repeater, a lever action weapon, which held twelve .44-caliber rimfire cartridges in a tube beneath the barrel. He knew it was seldom used since the Civil War, as the 1860 patented Spencer, loaded by seven-round tubes in the stock, was the weapon used mainly on the ranch and for hunting smaller game. Bullets fired by the Spencer could also be used in the .44-caliber revolver, which was preferred by many.

What was it doing here? Who had placed it in his bunk and why? His mind turned to Robert Running Fox. He had been certain the young buck he had aided had left, or had someone leave, the deer haunch. Since that time a buffalo heart and tongue, the cuts most prized by the Indians, had appeared on his doorstep, wrapped carefully in skin of the animal from which the parts obviously had been taken.

But why this? He examined the rifle carefully again. The cosmoline that covered it had been on it since leaving the factory. Was Running Fox trying to tell him something?

He heard Roy French coming in from the corral and, wrapping the weapon again in the deerskin, he shoved it back beneath his bunk. He would figure this out later. But at the present, he did not want French to know about it.

'Gets cool up here at night, don't it?' said Roy. He removed his outer garments and hat and, sighing, seated himself at the table.

'Hot during the summer, colder than blazes in the winter, I suspect,' said Josh. 'I've been here for two months so I don't rightly know about the winters yet.' He grinned. 'But, pardner, we will.'

Josh busied himself preparing a meal of steak, potatoes, some turnip greens the cook at the ranch had sent with them. That, with coffee and cold creek water, would be their meal for tonight. Tomorrow he would check their larder for something more.

'Tomorrow I will take you out on the range here and get you acquainted with the territory,' he told Roy as he worked. 'Then we are going to get to work and bring the beefs into the basin and drive them down for the roundup.'

Roy nodded and yawned. 'Sounds good to me. Shore is lonesome-like up here, ain't it?'

Josh dished up the food and sat down across the table from his new companion. 'It is that. But when we get busy dodging bad-tempered bulls and aggressive moma cows, we'll be so busy the lonesome will go away.'

French grinned and nodded and then dived into his meal. He was feeling the effects of having had no whiskey for two days. 'You got some liquor, Josh?' he asked. 'I'm needin' a little hair-of-the-dog.'

Josh shook his head. 'This is a working camp, Roy. No liquor except maybe for snakebites or bad scrapes. You'll be all right in a day or two,' he added. 'It takes a little time to work all that whiskey out of your system.'

French filled his mouth with steak and grunted.

Josh had been thinking about the new Henry Repeater rifle beneath his bunk. Why and how did it show up on his bunk? He had the answer a few days later.

French was gone to the far edge of the mesa to look for strayed beefs. He would be gone all day and Josh took the time to do work securing the shack before the winter snows came. He came around the corner of the cabin and jerked to a stop.

Robert Running Fox smiled at him and raised a hand. 'Howdy, my friend,' he said. Josh dropped the plank he was carrying and stepped up to shake the Indian's hand.

'It is good to see you, Running Fox,' Josh said seriously. 'You have recovered from your wounds?'

The Indian nodded. 'You saved my life, Joshua Cabel. I will always be indebted to you.' Running Fox eyed him thoughtfully. 'You found the rifle I left on your bunk?'

'I thought it might have been you who left it,' Josh

said. 'Where did you get such a gun, and absolutely new?'

'If you will come with me,' said the Indian, 'I will show you. It is very near.'

Josh saddled his horse and followed the Indian up a winding trail to the top of the bluff overlooking the cabin. They traveled along the bluff, following the contours of the ground, going higher and higher above the mesa. Finally they drew up at the lip of a sheer cliff. The Indian pointed down.

'There is the pueblo of my forefathers,' Running Fox said. 'The Old Ones, the Anasazi, built their homes here in the cliffs so long ago,' he threw his hands in the air and shrugged, 'they now live only in the memory-stories of our shamans, those who tell the history of our people.'

Josh dismounted and joined by Running Fox, moved to the edge of the cliff. Immediately below him, grass-covered and with some small trees growing from it, was the rooftop of one of the pueblos.

Josh looked at the Indian, a question in his eyes. Running Fox gestured to him and began to descend towards the pueblo, following a thin path along the edge of the cliff. 'Down here is what I wanted you to see,' he said.

From the rooftop of one crumbling pueblo onto another and another, through the walls of one that had given away to the erosion of the centuries, Josh followed the Indian. The sun was hot, the pueblo smelled of age and dust. Here and there Josh saw broken pottery. No one had been here for a long time, he surmised. He might be the only white man ever to see these ancient homes of a people who lived only in the stories told by old medicinemen to the youth of a vanishing people.

'In here,' Running Fox said. They had come down two tiers of the decaying, crumbling homes of Running Fox's ancestors. At about fifty feet down the face of the cliff, he led Josh into a larger, somewhat more secure pueblo. He pointed to a tarpaulin which covered a bulky stack of something. In one corner was another stack, much smaller and so covered.

Running Fox went to the larger stack in the center of the room and drew back one side of the covering. Beneath were wooden crates, stacked chest high. The Indian lifted the lid of one crate, obviously loosened before, and stepped back so Josh could see into the container.

Josh drew a deep breath. In the crate were rifles, the same .44-caliber Henry Repeater that Running Fox had brought to him. They were wrapped in oiled paper and undoubtedly still covered with the cosmoline that he had wiped from the rifle on his bunk. He straightened and looked at Running Fox.

'Who brought them here, and where are they going?' he asked the Indian. The purpose of the stash of weapons and ammunition was plain. The smaller stack in the corner was obviously cartridges for the rifles.

Running Fox eyed him thoughtfully. 'Sam Crawford knows who brought those weapons here, and he knows why. He also knows that at a certain time they will be picked up by Cheyenne who have heard the call of Sitting Bull, the great chief, to arm and drive all white men beyond the Father of Rivers.'

Josh sighed. He had known Crawford had something dwelling on his mind, otherwise why would he have sent Walker and Rush to kill Running Fox, whom he believed had learned of this cache of weapons? If these rifles got into the hands of the Cheyenne, and subsequently into Sitting Bull's hands, hundreds of soldiers would be slaughtered. Also ranchers and townspeople throughout the west.

Finally he nodded and drew the crate lid over the rifles and covered them with the tarpaulin. 'These must not be delivered or picked up by the Cheyenne,' he told Running Fox earnestly. 'I will contact the sheriff at Colorado City. He will see that the rifles are never given to Sitting Bull.'

At the top of the cliff, above the pueblos, Josh paused before mounting his horse. 'Running Fox,' he said, 'you have been a friend not only to me, but to many in the future, for exposing this secret of Crawford's.' He reached out and the two clasped wrists in the Indian fashion of the handshake.

'You be very careful, my friend,' said Running Fox. 'There are those who will kill just to have this secret left untold. From now on ride with eyes seeing all.' With that he mounted his painted cayuse and rode away without looking back.

With narrowed eyes Ned Walker, hidden in a dry wash on the top of the cliff and near the trail along which Josh had ridden to inspect the pueblo, watched as the cowboy and Indian parted, each going their separate ways.

Waiting a half hour he hurried down the cliff into the room where the weapons were stored. His lips compressed in anger and frustration when he saw the tracks in the dust and that the tarp had been removed and replaced. Cursing beneath his breath, he pulled back the tarp and saw immediately a crate had been opened and one of the weapons taken.

The secret was no longer a secret. The Cheyenne had to be told and come to receive the weapons. And Josh Cabel had to be stopped. Otherwise he would go to the sheriff or even a Federal Marshal and report the cache.

Eleven

Sheriff Mark Spears eyed Josh Cabel as the cowboy related what he had seen in the pueblos on the backside of the Bar-C ranch. Only the tightening and work of the muscles in his jaws betrayed any emotion of the lawman. Finally he sighed and leaned back in his chair.

'I know Robert Running Fox. I didn't know anything had happened to him. He's never been in any kind of trouble that I know of.' He fell silent, contemplative. Then continued slowly. 'I've known Sam Crawford ever since he came here after the war. I would never have suspected him of being involved in any kind of outlawry as this. Damn . . . passin' on guns to the Injuns.' He eyed Josh again. 'An' you believe Running Fox's story?'

'Sheriff, I saw the cache of guns and ammo, and I have one of the rifles in my cabin if you want to come out and see it. I can take you to the pueblo where the guns are stored.'

Mark Spears was an honest sheriff. He had begun his trade after returning home from the Civil War. He had briefly worked with the Rangers in Texas, along the Mexican border, where outlaws raided cattle from ranches near the Rio Grande, drove them across the river and sold them to willing buyers.

Leaving this he had been sheriff in a town in Wyoming Territory and hearing that a lawman was needed in Colorado City, he had applied for the job. The town fathers quickly elected him for their need, and for the fact that his honesty and strength against those disturbing the peace had preceded him. He had been in Colorado City long enough to let the lawless know that he would tolerate no shooting and that unruly drunks would be jailed forthwith. He liked the town, liked his job, and now was deeply disturbed to hear that a man he had felt straight was dealing in an illegal arms trade at a time when Indian trouble seemed to be rising on the horizon. He shook his head.

'I'll come to the ranch in a day or so,' he said, 'and ask for you. I'll come on out to the mesa and you can take me to the cache.' He eyed Josh thoughtfully. 'Talk has it that you're lookin' for someone . . . a man named Baker, John Baker?'

Josh nodded. 'I was told back in Kansas that Baker had come west. Later I was informed that he might be in Laramie, Wyoming, or here or in Denver.' He rose from the chair, picking up his hat from the corner of the desk. 'I'd like to ask around town, if you don't mind.'

'I don't mind,' the sheriff said. 'Just be careful and watch your trail. Someone might hear what you're after and be layin' up for you.' The sheriff went with him to the door. 'Care to tell me why you're lookin' so hard for this feller?'

Josh turned to face the sheriff. 'He murdered my parents and sister in cold blood,' he gritted, his eyes hot and narrowed. 'I know you allow no gunplay in your town, but if I find him here . . . I'll kill him and take the consequences.' His cold stare met the eyes of the sheriff unflinchingly.

The sheriff met his gaze eye to eye. 'You do that and I'll be seein' you,' he said quietly. 'You kill him anywhere in this county, and I'll be after you. You'd best let me handle it, if you find him.'

Josh looked at him a long moment and without speaking again left the office. Leading his horse to the livery across the street, he saw the animal in the hands of a stableman, who for two bits offered a nosebag of grain for the horse, and for another two bits a good rub down and some hay. Josh paid and left the livery.

At the Red Dog Saloon, where he had sat with Roy French and talked him into taking a regular job, Josh ordered a beer and with a handful of crackers went to a table at the side of the room and sat down.

The beer gone, the saloon keeper, seeing the empty mug, signaled to Josh, his eyebrows raised in question. Josh nodded. After a few weeks of hard work, rounding up the cattle on the mesa, it was nice to relax and forget the bovine smells for a while.

The barkeep was not busy, it being the lull time before the late afternoon and evening customers arrived. He placed a full pitcher of beer on the table and drawing up a chair, sat down facing Josh.

'Cabel, ain't it?'

Josh nodded. 'Thanks for the beer. It hits the spot.'

The barkeep shrugged. 'Obliged,' he said. 'It's my job. Say, ain't you that cowhand who scrapped with Roy French?'

'Yep.' Josh sipped his beer.

'Got him a job on the Bar-C Ranch, I hear. How's he doin'?'

'Roy's doing fine,' said Josh. 'He's a good worker. Someone just had to get him settled down and burn the whiskey out of his system.'

The barkeep leaned on his elbows and eyed Josh carefully. 'I seem to recollect you asking about a man here in the saloon when you first came into town. Baker, wasn't it?'

Josh nodded. 'Yes. Have you had anyone in here by that name?'

The barkeep shook his head. 'Can't say I have. But there's been a feller 'quirin' about you. Kinda small guy, with a bad right hand. Wore his gun on his right side, butt forward like a cross-draw.' He watched Josh for any reaction.

Josh went cold. Arley Hawkins, here? How had he followed Josh, for Cabel had been many places asking his question about Baker?

'What did he want? Anything special?' he asked the bartender.

'Well . . . he asked about the same man you did . . . Baker. And he acted like he knowed you.'

Josh nodded grimly. 'He knows me all right. He's a hardcase wanting to make a name for himself as a shootist. He and I got into a little argument and it resulted in him losing most of the fingers on his right hand.' Josh fell silent, thinking of Hawkins, wondering how he had managed to show up in Colorado City, at this particular time.

'Oh, he asked about you,' the barkeep said. 'But he's been quiet. No gunplay, no hard drinkin'. Just hangin' around and watchin', seems like.'

*

Sheriff Spears showed up on the Bar-C Ranch when everyone but the cook was out gathering beef for the roundup. When asked about Josh and where he might be, he was directed to the mesa meadows. When Roy French dropped by the cabin after a morning of razing wily beefs from impossible brakes, the sheriff and Josh were preparing to ride out to the pueblos.

'You stick around the cabin this afternoon,' Josh suggested to Roy, 'while I show the sheriff about the range here.' Roy shrugged. It was none of his business and besides, he was busy fixing himself a beef and mustard sandwich for lunch.

Mark Spears eyed the stacked crates of rifles and the stack of ammunition. 'When will it be picked up?' he asked. 'Did Running Fox have any idea?'

'He just said it wouldn't be long.'

The sheriff eyed the sheer bluff above the pueblo. 'I think there's an old wagon trail up there,' he pointed to the sheer bluff above the pueblo. 'They will have to bring in pack mules, and maybe a wagon, to haul all this out of here.' He paused. 'Did Running Fox say when they might be comin' after the cache?'

Josh shook his head. 'He just said he suspected they would be coming soon.'

The sheriff left and French went out to a nearby meadow to rope and bring in one of their mounts, turning one loose to graze. Josh took a bucket and went to the creek bank, above a hole of clear water and dipped the utensil in the cool, flowing liquid.

As he raised with the filled bucket, there was a sharp resounding boom and lightning struck his head. As he blacked out his final thought was on Arley Hawkins. Spinning darkness enfolded him, and he fell, the water spilling over him.

Roy French found him an hour later. He heard the sharp echo of a rifle being fired, seeming to come from the direction of the cabin. He raced his horse back to the cabin and saw the dark, unmoving form of his partner near the creek bank. Fearing the worst, he knelt over the body and touched Josh's throat, searching for a pulse. He felt the throb of the heart, steady but weak. He ain't dead, French mused, but he's hurt bad. Real bad.

Gathering Josh up in huge arms he carried his partner to the cabin and placed him on a bunk. Who had done this to Cabel? He shook his head. Never mind, help must be gotten, or his partner would die.

Twelve

Les Parker saw Ned Walker and Tim Rush go past the corrals and ride up toward the main house. They trailed a pack horse loaded with gear. Apparently they were on their way out of the country. His face tightened. Good riddance, he thought. Should have run them out long before this.

The two did not stop to talk with Parker, even though he left the tack shed where he had been working, and walked toward them. They ignored his approach and continued to draw up before the main house. Walker dismounted and stepped up on the veranda, knocked at the door.

A maid opened the door. 'I'd like to see Sam Crawford,' Ned drawled.

'Just a moment.' The woman, wife of one of the older hands on the ranch, disappeared into the house. In a few minutes Crawford came to the door. Seeing the two before him, he scowled. 'I thought you two were gone,' he growled. 'What are you doin' here? I thought you were out of the country by now.'

Ned shook his head. 'Nope. We just finished a job

for you. We think you owe us some money now
because of it.'

Crawford glared. 'Get outta here! I don't . . . .'

Walker held up a hand. 'Cool down, friend. Do
you want me to blurt out what we know and what we
did, so's everyone can hear us? I think you'd better
ask us in so we kin talk quiet-like.'

Crawford narrowed his eyes to ivy slits. His heavy
face hardened. 'I have nothing to talk about. Now
get off my ranch!'

Walker leaned closer until his breath, laden with
the stink of tobacco and bad teeth, washed into
Crawford's nostrils. 'You wanted Josh Cabel outta th'
way? Well, we done took him out. Now, we want to be
paid for doin' somethin' you didn't have the guts to
do.' He leered. 'Your secret's safe with us, so long as
the reward is good.'

Crawford eyed him narrowly, dislike mirrored
upon his face. Finally he stepped aside and motioned
for them to come in. At that moment Parker
appeared behind them and Crawford motioned for
him to come in, also.

'They say they killed Cabel,' he muttered as Parker
stepped past him. 'I want you here when they tell
their story. See if you think they're lyin'.'

The two men had stepped into Crawford's office.
Crawford and Parker entered and Parker closed the
door behind them. The owner of the Bar-C Ranch
dropped into a chair behind his desk and looked at
the two dirty, ragged men standing before him.

'Is he gonna listen to what we have to say?' asked
Rush.

Crawford scowled at him. 'Les Parker has been
with me far longer than you. I have no secrets from

him. Now, tell me what happened.'

Walker related how, hidden, they had watched Josh Cabel go to the pueblo where the guns were stashed. They had lain in wait near his shack and when 'the dummy', as they called Roy French, went to the meadows to catch up a mount, they had waited until Josh appeared from the cabin. He went to the creek and, dipping up a bucket of water, started back to the shack. Walker shot him from behind.

'Did you examine to see if he was really dead?' asked Parker, disgust showing on his face. If there was anything worse than a horse thief, it was a back-shooter.

Walker leered at him and Rush snorted with derision. 'Miss at fifty yards? Walker? Naw, he was dead all right. We could tell by the way he fell.'

Crawford looked at Parker. 'D'you think they're tellin' it straight?' he asked the foreman. 'Or is this all made up?'

'How long did you wait before you left?' Parker asked Rush. For some reason he trusted Rush more than Walker.

Rush shook his head. 'We knowed he was dead. We left, thinkin' French would be back soon.'

Crawford chewed his lower lip for a long moment, going over what had been claimed. Finally he sighed. Reaching into a lower drawer of his desk, he brought out a small metal box and, opening it, counted out two hundred dollars and handed it to Parker. 'You pay 'em off and get 'em off my ranch.' He glared at Rush and Walker. 'I never want to set eyes on either of you again.' He looked at Parker. 'Get them out of here!'

*

The next day Parker entered his boss's office and laid the two hundred dollars on the desk. 'They're gone, outta the way,' he said, with a significant look at Crawford.

Crawford nodded and shoved the money back to the foreman. 'You keep it,' he said. 'You earned it.'

It was months later that the skeletons of two men were discovered in a small coulée off the road leading into Colorado City from the Bar-C Ranch. A cowboy, searching the brush for some errant beefs found the bones, some covered by blown sand or washed over by rain. He stared and shrugged. A couple of fellows got a mad on and had a shoot-out, he reasoned. Neither of them won. With this he moved on and never thought of it again.

Thirteen

French hurried to the creek and dipped up a bucket of water. Racing back to the cabin, he entered and slid to a stop. He dropped the bucket of water and fumbled for his gun.

The Indian bending over Cabel glanced at him. 'I am Robert Running Fox,' he said, turning his eyes back to the white face of his friend. 'Someone tried to kill Josh Cabel?' He turned Josh's head and stared stoically at the bleeding gash over the left ear, reaching around to the back of the head.

'Who'er you?' French asked. 'Yes, someone shot Josh. I heard the shot, a rifle, I think, and come on in. I found him down by the creek.'

The Indian nodded. 'I owe Josh Cabel my life,' he said. 'I will take him to my village and care for him. He will not die.' He stepped to the door and whistled softly. In a few moments two Indian braves appeared and entered, looking questioningly at Running Fox.

Running Fox spoke to them rapidly in their tongue. 'This white-eye is my friend. Build a travois quickly. We must take him to our village so our shaman can say prayers over him and make the medicine smoke.' He turned to Roy French. 'We are

99

taking him to my village. We need one of your horses to pull a travois.'

French nodded and left for the corral. In a few minutes he led a horse to the front of the cabin. The Indians had stripped two slim poles of limbs and bark and fashioned them together with blankets from the cabin. In a few minutes Josh Cabel, still unconscious, was transported away from the cabin.

Before leaving, Robert Running Fox spoke to French. 'If our friend was shot by any of Crawford's men, they will come looking for the body. If so, you tell them that you were out on the range working the cattle for the roundup, which I know will be soon. You found Josh Cabel gone and know nothing about his disappearing. If you do this, you should be safe. I know the reason Josh Cabel was shot. But you apparently do not. It is better, now, that you know nothing.'

French's slow mind turned this over and he nodded. 'I just keep on workin' until Josh comes back, eh? I can do that. Josh is a good man – I don't know why anyone would shoot him.'

Running Fox nodded gravely and, turning, followed the travois into the darkness.

'What do you mean? The body was gone an' French didn't know where?' asked Crawford, looking worriedly into Les Parker's face. 'What's happenin' here?'

Parker shook his head. 'French said he came in and Josh wasn't here. Someone had to have come and taken Cabel away.'

'Do you think French was truthful? Could he and Cabel have discovered the cache of arms together and be planning to do something with the guns?' Crawford asked. He thought for a moment. 'Or maybe Walker and Rush lied about it.'

'Either is possible, but I don't think that is what happened. If he was shot, then I think Cabel must have just been stunned. He came to and got a horse and left camp, for one of the horses is gone. It all happened while French was away from the cabin.'

Crawford was silent a long time. He slowly tamped tobacco into a pipe and spent moments getting it drawing just right. Finally he leaned back in his chair and looked at Parker.

'We've got to get those rifles out of there. Get word to that crooked Indian agent in Denver and tell him the rifles have to go now. We can't take a chance that Cabel is alive and he and French are planning to get away with the cache for whatever reason.'

Les frowned. 'It'll take at least a week for them to receive a message and get down here.' He thought for a moment and nodded. 'I'll send a telegram from Colorado City tomorrow.'

'Be careful what you say,' Crawford cautioned. 'Word it so they get the message, but no one else could read the telegram and know what it was about.'

Josh Cabel had the feeling he was floating through a smoke-filled tunnel. Dim light swirled about him. He was warm, he was hot, he felt smothered. The light grew and the swirling stopped, the smoky feeling lessened. He opened his eyes.

He saw above him a ceiling held up by long poles and coming together at the top. The poles were covered by a heavy material. The material was open at the top and as his vision cleared, he noticed a small swirl of smoke escaping through the opening.

A small hand touched his face and he tried to turn his head. A sharp pain shot through his head and he gasped. A voice spoke to him in English words, not fully connected yet making sense.

'You wake now. Good.' The voice was quiet and melodic. The hand that had touched him was withdrawn and his eyes focused upon dark features, female features, eyes deep black and concerned. Two braids lay across the chest which was gently rounded beneath soft deerskin.

'Where . . . where am I?' Josh tried to ask, had to clear his throat and begin again.

'You safe now. Not worry. I go tell my brother you awake. You rest. I be back soon.'

She rose lithely and smiled down at him gravely, then left him. A tepee, he thought. A hogan, no . . . a summer tepee. They went into hogans when it became cold . . . Indian woman . . . he was . . . he drifted away into a quiet sleep again.

He sensed movement about him and awakened again. At his slight movement and opening of his eyes, someone came to his side. He looked up into the dark, sharp features . . . of his Indian friend, Robert Running Fox.

'Good. You are really awake now,' Running Fox lowered to a cross-legged seat beside Josh's pallet. 'You have been hurt pretty bad. But you are stronger now.'

Josh smiled weakly, making certain he did not move his head as he had when he was awake earlier. 'How long have I been here?' he asked.

The Indian held up four fingers. 'You have been asleep four days and nights. You were shot in the head, a glancing blow, but it knocked you senseless. I was just coming down the cliff back of your cabin when I heard the shot. By the time I got to the cabin, your friend, French, has found you and put you into your bunk.'

'French . . . is he all right? He wasn't shot, too?'

The Indian shook his head. 'No, your friend is fine. He knows you are here. I will send one from my village to tell him you are awake now.'

Josh tried to rise, but the pain in his head came again. He gasped and sank back on the pallet. Running Fox shook his head. 'You are not ready to get up. Tomorrow, maybe you can get up and walk outside awhile. But you have been badly hurt and need to be quiet and get your strength back.'

Josh lay back and sighed and then said, 'I'm hungry . . . in fact I'm starving.'

Running Fox laughed softly. 'This is the best sign of all. My sister, Whispering Dawn, will care for you. She will make you some soup and feed you. Her man, Spotted Horse, is away on a hunting trip. She has no children at the moment but carries one under her skirt.' He smiled. 'She is a good woman; we are very close.'

Josh nodded, feeling very weak. He was aware that he had been seriously wounded. But knowing the sheriff would be enquiring about him, he was anxious to be on his feet and working. Nevertheless, he knew his friend was correct. He had to rest several hours and then see if he could function.

He looked up at Running Fox. 'Is the bullet still in my head?' he asked.

The Indian shook his head. 'No. It glanced as it hit, going around a few inches beneath the scalp and

went out, leaving a large tear in the skin. Ruined a
perfectly good scalp,' he grinned. 'You are safe now
– no self-respecting Indian would want that scalp on
his lance.' Josh laughed and then winced as pain
lanced through his head again.

'Rest now,' Running Fox told him. 'My sister will
be in soon with a bowl of deermeat stew, with some
onions and other herbs in it. They are all good for
you.' He nodded to Josh and left the tepee.

Elmo Sanders was the Indian agent for the territory.
He was a political appointee. Basically a dishonest
man, after he took over the agency it was not long
before he was following the action of many such
agents appointed to safeguard the welfare of the
Indians under their jurisdiction. Cattle brought in
for reservations, clothing for the individuals, foodstuffs for the long winters for the non-hunters – these
were siphoned off by the agents, who then pocketed
the money. It was illegal and punishable when
detected, but the activity was rampant as the reservations grew. Church organizations in the east sent
barrels of foodstuffs, bales of clothing, and many
other items which, intended for the welfare of the
Indians, never touched the life of the redman, or if
so, only in scarcity.

In this particular action, where the weapons were
stored in the ancient pueblo on the Bar-C Ranch, he
had not yet made firm commitment with traders for
them. He knew, when he received the telegram, that
it was imperative the weapons be moved.

Hiring some roustabouts and two wagons from
Colorado City, he led them to the pueblos, and
directed the loading of the cache.

The wagons loaded, he mounted his horse and led the way along the ancient trail above the cliff dwellings. Turning a bend in the trail, he drew his mount to a quick stop. Sitting upon his horse in the middle of the trail was Sheriff Mark Spears, eyes narrowed and face stern, his rifle lifted slowly and centered upon the chest of the Indian agent.

'Get down off your hoss, an' drop your gunbelt,' Spears offered, his voice grating. 'And tell the rest of your gang to do the same.'

Elmo Sanders looked at the sheriff and sneered. 'One man, orderin' seven men around? Nothin' doin', Sheriff. Ride on out of here. I'm coming through.' Sanders started to touch spurs to his mount.

Spears raised his hand and then said, 'Look around you, friend, an' do what I tell you.'

The Indian agent turned his eyes toward the cliff side of the trail and saw five deputy sheriffs whose rifles bore down upon him and his workers. He jerked about, pulling his mount away from the cliff, and blanched, stopping the horse. Six deputies rose slowly from behind boulders and bushes. He and those with him were covered with twelve rifles, held by grim-faced men.

Fourteen

Josh Cabel spent two more days in the Indian camp, beyond his awakening from the glancing blow to the head by Ned Walker's fired bullet. These two days he spent becoming more acquainted with Whispering Dawn, the beautiful sister of Running Fox. He was invited into the tepee of the tribal chief, Strong Bull, and smoked the pipe of friendship with him and his council.

On the seventh day following his being brought to the encampment, he mounted the horse from his own corral that had pulled the travois holding his inert body. He paused, looking down at Running Fox and Whispering Dawn.

'You have been friends to me,' he said. 'I owe you my life. I have rested in the peaceful environment of your people, and would like to know that, from time to time, I may return to be among my friends.'

Running Fox nodded and his sister smiled, lowering her face and then looking at Josh and smiling. 'You are always welcome,' Running Fox said. 'You are welcome in my camp and in my tepee.'

Raising his hand in a farewell salute, Josh rode out

106

of the Indian camp, beyond the circle of tepees, stretched deer hides on aspen frames, smoldering fires and yapping dogs. For all the strangeness and noise, it had been a peaceful place, among friendly and gracious people. He knew he left friendship and respect behind him.

It was coming on dusk when he arrived back at the cabin. A thin swirl of smoke rose from the chimney. A feeling of happiness swelled through him. He noticed the increase of beefs in the meadows beyond the house. His partner, Roy French, had been working.

He dismounted at the corral back of the house and French, coming from the shack, having heard the sound of hoofs, approached him with a wide grin on his face.

'By Golly,' he said, laughing, 'you made it back, an' fer as I kin see, all in one piece.'

They clasped hands and Roy pounded Josh's back until he had to pull back. 'I'm glad to be back in one piece, Roy,' Josh said. 'But the pieces might fly apart if you don't stop pounding me.'

Roy grinned, and proceeded to help Josh with the tack and with rubbing down the horse before turning it into the corral.

'Since you have been gone,' he said as he carried the saddle into the shed, 'Les Parker has been here. He was pretty worried about you, an' so was I. Then the Injun come with th' word that you was all right. When I saw all that blood on the ground by the creek I was shore you was a goner.'

'I'm all right now, Roy. There's some things going on I'll tell you about. But right now we have to get the beefs down into the flats for the roundup.' They talked into the night, drinking coffee, laced with a shot of brandy now and then. Roy rolled into his blankets and was asleep in moments. But it was not his snores that kept Josh awake for a long time.

Les Parker showed up as Josh and French were driving the last of the cattle off the mesa and lining them up on the trail to the flats. At the sight of Josh, he jerked his horse still, and stared at the cowboy. Josh rode up to him, seeing the blanched face and questioning eyes.

'Howdy, Les,' he said. 'We ought to have these critters to the flats by dark. Have the rest of the range beefs been driven in?'

Parker nodded, his eyes on Josh's face. He breathed a deep breath, color coming back to his face. 'I figured you were a goner, Cabel,' he said. 'There was blood on the ground and no body. I nosed around and saw some moccasin tracks. I figured that Indian, Running Fox, had come and shot you for some reason or another.'

Josh shook his head. 'To the contrary, Les. Robert Running Fox probably saved my life. Someone shot me in the head. The Indian just happened along and took me to the camp up above the cliff houses. I been back and working for a couple of days.'

Les swung his horse around beside Josh's, and proceeded to help them continue the drive, arriving at the roundup flats at dusk. Herds of cattle were formed here and there, kept in place by cowboys from various ranches. The cattle roamed the ranges and became mixed. Hands from nearby ranches aided in the roundup and branding, cutting their own branded beefs from the main herd and holding them aside.

It was the last day of the roundup that Saralou rode up and sought Cabel. He was finishing working with a young bull and, seeing the animal altered and branded, stepped back and saw the girl waiting, smiling down at him.

'Hello, Josh Cabel. I'm glad to see you. I heard you were hurt.' She dismounted and, ground reining her mount, walked to him. She looked into his eyes and he blushed at the soft expression on her face.

'I had an accident,' he told her, removing his hat and wiping his face with his bandanna. 'Nothing real bad.'

'I'm glad,' she said. 'I came out here for two reasons. One to see if you were here and all right. I've been worried. The second reason is that Sheriff Spears of Colorado City sent word he wanted you to come in and talk with him.' She eyed him with concern on her face. 'Are you in trouble, Josh? If so, maybe my father can help you.'

Josh shook his head. 'I'm in no trouble that I know of,' he said. 'Send someone to the sheriff that I'll be there in a day or two. The roundup is just about over.'

She nodded. Then reached out and touched his hand. 'I had one more reason for coming.' She paused and then continued, a blush slowly coming over her features. She lowered her eyes. 'The roundup dance will be in two weeks in Colorado City. I'd like very much to go, if I can find someone to take me.'

Josh looked at her solemnly and bowed. 'Ma'am, I'd be pleasured to escort such a pretty lady to the dance.'

She looked into his face with soft eyes and a slow, sweet smile. 'It will be my pleasure, also,' she said softly. Then, looking at Josh one more time, she mounted her horse and galloped out of the roundup area.

'We were there when a feller named Elmo Sanders showed up with a gang of no-goods to take the rifles and ammo,' Sheriff Spears said. He and Josh sat in late afternoon shade before the sheriff's office. 'Sanders is an Indian agent for the territory. He raised hailcolumbia. But I put them all in jail. Sanders hired hisself a lawyer an' got out on a misdemeanor, or some such crazy thing. The rest I kept in jail until I can get a Deputy US Marshal down here and turn the case over to him.'

'How about Sanders? Did he talk any?' asked Josh.

The sheriff nodded. 'The Bar-C foreman, Parker, is mixed up in it somehow. And if so, then Crawford's shirt-tail ain't clean. I mean to talk with them as soon as I can, before the marshal gets here.'

Josh shook his head. 'I would never have thought it of either of them,' he said softly. 'The amount they would receive from the sale of the guns is nothing to what Crawford will get when he ships his beef in a few weeks. Why take a chance like that, knowing it's illegal?'

The sheriff looked at him, pulling slowly on his pipe. Smoke pluming about his head, he answered slowly. 'There's no answer to something like that,' he said. 'Maybe it's just the extra money. I heered that Crawford borrowed considerable on his holdings. Maybe he's in a money pinch.' He shook his head, holding the pipe in his hands. 'Whatever, I agree wih you, why take the chance, knowing it's not only agin th' law, but actually immoral, when you think of the soldiers and innocent ranchers that could have been killed with them guns.'

Josh decided to stay the night in Colorado City. There was a saloon in the center of town that sold reasonably good liquor and excellently brewed beer. Besides, he had been paid for the roundup, and decided to play a few hands of poker. Maybe he might drop the name of John Baker at the table, casually and get some information he did not have. He could not shake the feeling that Baker had settled somewhere around Colorado City or Denver, which was an easy three-days ride on horseback.

He entered the Colorado Emporium, as the saloon was called, and going to the bar, ordered a beer. He leaned against the bar, enjoying the taste after long days working cattle in dirt and heat. At a table against the far wall, four men of the city were enjoying a game of poker.

It had grown dark outside, and the bartender moved about, lighting kerosene reflector lamps. Josh watched him, and paid no attention when the batwing doors swung open. Spurs jingled across the sawdust floor then ceased. Josh sensed a quietness in the room and, taking his attention from the poker game, turned his head.

Arley Hawkins pushed back his hat and leered at Josh. 'Well, well,' he chortled. 'I've finally run into you. I knew it would happen, sooner or later.'

Josh eyed the man, noting the deformed right hand, the gun now holstered on the right hip, toward the front of the belly, butt forward. He has taught himself to cross-draw, Josh thought.

'Why do you want to run me down?' asked Cabel, stepping away from the bar, freeing his right arm to hang loosely at his side. 'I have nothing to do with you.'

'Aw, yes you have,' sneered Hawkins. 'I larned something after you shot up my hand. I'm ready for you now an' tonight is going to be the time! But before we draw, I've got some news for you.'

Cabel eased away from the bar. The barkeep spoke sharply, 'Stop it right there!' he said. 'There'll be no gunplay in my place. I've had enough trouble with the sheriff as it is.'

'Shut your yap!' Hawkins snarled at the barkeep. 'I got somethin' to tell this yahoo.' He turned his attention back to Josh Cabel.

'You still lookin' fer that feller, John Baker?' He peered from under his hat brim.

'I am,' said Josh shortly.

Hawkins threw back his head and laughed. 'Why you have been huntin' for Baker all this time . . . some hunter you are. You've been here for a whole season an' all the time you've been workin' . . . .'

The darkness beyond the batwinged doors was broken by the red flame of a rifle shot. Hawkins stiffened, his mouth opened and blood poured down over his chin and onto his chest. His eyes bulged and he stared at Josh with a slowly developing look of death. He swayed, clutched at a nearby chairback, and then collapsed onto the sawdust floor of the saloon, his body twitching in the last throes of death.

Fifteen

Les Parker occupied a chair in Sam Crawford's untidy office. His face was haggard and his eyes dull with want of rest. He was bone tired from the hard work of the roundup, and from a long trip he had just completed. He eyed his boss warily.

'It's gone, Sam. Every round, every piece. There's wagon tracks at the top of the cliff coming and going. And today, in Colorado City, I learned what happened to it all.'

Sam Crawford eyed his foreman. He sensed that whatever news Parker had was far from positive. He leaned back in his creaky desk chair and lit a cigar. Through the smoke he nodded to his foreman.

'Well, don't sit there like a stump,' he growled. 'I can't read yore mind. What did you learn in town?'

Parker hesitated and then shook his head. 'Sam, the sheriff somehow got wind of the cache. He was there when the Indian agent, Sanders, showed up. Sanders had come runnin' when he got my telegram. The sheriff had been informed of what was goin' on an' was waitin'. He jailed the men the agent had hired and Sanders, too. Sanders is out on bail: the rest are still in the jug.'

Sam Crawford was silent. His face flushed in anger and then paled as he thought over what Parker told him. The loss of the guns was a blow, for he had put a great amount of cash into the project. It was to be a one-time deal, no questions asked, and his return would lift him from debts this season's sale of cattle would not completely cover.

'Did the Indian agent talk? Did he spill his guts to the sheriff?'

'He musta said somethin'. The sheriff told a deputy that he was goin' to get a US Marshal down to look into it all.'

The two men were silent for a long time. Crawford finally stirred He looked with worried eyes at the foreman. 'Les, I think you'd better take a ride up to Denver and make shore that agent keeps his mouth shut.'

Parker stared at him. 'That's a week, there an' back,' he said. 'Are you shore you want me to go?'

Crawford sighed and nodded. 'Yeah, Les. You had better have a talk with him.' He leaned forward and stared at Parker. 'You make shore he don't talk to anyone else about this mixup.' Then, as an after-thought, 'What happened to the guns? Where did they end up? In the jail's tack shed?' He grimaced at the thought.

Parker shook his head. 'Nope. He give it to the army at Fort Collins. The colonel was happy to have a hundred new rifles and ammo to go with them.'

Crawford grunted. 'I heard there was a shootin' in Colorado City the other evening. What do you know about it?'

Les Parker grimaced. 'No more than you do, I guess. Some cowhand was bracin' Josh Cabel an' about to draw on him, when someone from the street shot him in the back with a rifle. Killed him instantly.' He hesitated and then continued. 'Seems he was about to tell Cabel where the man is that Josh has been huntin'. Name of Baker.'

Crawford eyed him levelly. 'Guess it was for the best,' he said. He stood and stretched. 'Get on yore way to Denver come light,' he said. 'The quicker Sanders is taken care of, the better it'll be for all concerned.'

In Denver, Deputy US Marshal Jackson Taylor Harrison studied the telegram that had arrived at his desk the previous evening. 'Always something,' he thought. Rustlers, wanted gangs, Indian trouble. Now some rancher hiding weapons that may have been intended for trading to the tribes. He shook his head. Reckon I'll just have to get down there and see what it is all about.

Jackson Taylor Harrison was named by his father, a former member of Zachary Taylor's small army of five thousand men who fought at Buena Vista. His grandfather had marched on New Orleans with Andrew Jackson. Carrying names with such an aura of history, the marshal sought to live up to them by serving in his present occupation, seeing that law and order might become more precious in this wild, wide and outlaw-ridden west. It was becoming better. Towns had honest lawmen; more and more men, coming out of the Civil War, were seeking the protection of the law. He felt deeply that rules of law and order would be followed and adhered to in the future. He sighed, the sooner the better, he thought, and reread the telegram from Colorado City. He would take the train down in the next day or two.

In the meantime he would check in on the Indian agent Sanders. More than once he had been called upon to investigate rumors surrounding the activities of the agent. This would probably be like all the others. All wind and smoke, but no real fire.

Sanders lived in a small house on the outskirts of Denver. He was unmarried, but there was always a 'housekeeper' present, and friends and acquaintances raised their eyebrows at her youthfulness and forwardness of attitude. No self-respecting woman with such becoming and early years would be a 'live-in' housekeeper unless there was something more in the wind than a place to sleep and food to eat, with only a small salary paid now and then.

The house was set apart from several others on a short street, off one of the main streets of the town. No one saw the man ride up and who, tying his horse to the rail in front, went to the door and knocked.

Nor did they pay attention to the shot that sounded up and down the small street. Sanders fell back into the room, astonishment crossing his face. He coughed, blood gushing from his throat. The man in the doorway watched his final throes and hearing the hurrying footsteps of the live-in housekeeper, softly closed the door. Moments later the quiet hoofbeats of his departure were covered by the screams at the Sanders house.

Marshal Harrison saw the announcement of the death of Sanders in the local newspaper. The cause of death was a gunshot wound in the chest. The local constabulary had been unable to apprehend the assailant of Sanders, the housekeeper being no help, as she had been bathing at the time and came into the room to see her benefactor dead upon the floor.

He visited the home and talked with the woman, but got no further information than had the local constable. He and the sheriff of the territory talked, but came up with no solution. This was on his mind when he boarded the train to Colorado City.

Sheriff Spears met the marshal at the depot, taking him to the Colorado Emporium for a beer to cut the dust from his throat and relax for a few minutes before getting into the reason for the marshal's visit. When Spears mentioned that the Bar-C Ranch owner and foreman were under suspicion of trafficking illegally in weapons, the marshal shook his head.

'Sam Crawford would be the last I would suspect of being involved in such a thing,' he said. 'I knew Sanders had a reputation, but that he was a gun-runner for arming the tribes never entered my mind. That he and such an upstanding person as Crawford would be in cahoots together surprises me.'

The two officers of the law talked for a long while, examining the information they had on the illegal traffic in weapons, involving Crawford and Parker, now that Sanders was dead.

'It appears someone decided to take Sanders out of the picture before he could be pressured to tell all he knew,' Marshal Harrison said. 'Good riddance to a bad actor, but now we have to deal with the rest of those guilty.'

Sheriff Spears nodded. 'I think we'd better face Crawford with what we know and see how he takes it. The sooner the better.'

*

As the sheriff and marshal decided the direction to go, Parker had arrived back at the Bar-C Ranch and went directly to Crawford's office.

'It's taken care of,' he told his boss. 'Now, if we can get Cabel to keep his mouth shut, we'll be in the clear,' he told Crawford.

'What was that about Josh?' Saralou stood in the doorway of the office. 'Is he in trouble of some kind?'

Crawford shook his head. 'Nothin' you need to bother yore purty head about, honey. Just man talk. Josh has been workin' hard gettin' the line shack ready for winter up on the mesa, and Parker and me was just discussin' it.'

She smiled and leaned against the doorjamb. 'Josh is going to take me to the dance Saturday,' she said dreamily. 'He's the best dancer I ever knew.'

Crawford frowned and then cleared his face and smiled. 'That's nice, honey, real nice. I guess you'll be safe with Cabel. I'll talk to him before you leave.'

She tossed her head. 'Don't you say anything to him to change his mind,' she said, coming into the room and leaning over the desk. She leaned down and kissed his cheek. 'He's very nice and I like him a lot.'

She danced from the room. Crawford looked at Parker and sighed. 'Good lord,' he said. 'She's in love with him. Now what are we goin' to do?'

Parker smiled, his eyes glinting with a hidden evil. 'Leave it to me, boss,' he said. 'I'll arrange it so Cabel will be happy to leave the Bar-C.'

A few minutes later Parker talked with two men, one a huge lout who took the foreman's orders without question. They caught up horses and a few minutes later struck out toward the mesa. Parker watched them go, a grim smile on his lips. Cabel would be doing no dancing come Saturday night!

Sixteen

Josh watched Roy French approaching from the corral where he had just attended to the horse he had ridden in from the range. During the two months Roy had worked with him, the big man had slimmed down, losing the fat brought on his wide frame by poor food and constant drinking of beer and whiskey. His face, neck and hands were tanned a dark brown, his eyes were bright and clear. Roy French had benefited greatly from his relationship with Josh Cabel.

Coming up to the creek-stone slab that formed the step before the door of the cabin, he paused and, removing his hat, wiped sweat from his forehead.

'Josh we're gettin' company. Two riders. Was you expectin' someone from the ranch to come?'

'Nope.' Josh shook his head. 'Could you recognize either of them? Or their horses?'

'Not the riders, but I do think I remember one of the hosses. A piebald rid by one of the boys from the ranch.'

As the riders crossed the creek in front of the cabin, Josh recognized a big cowboy. 'Hoss' Younger, called so by his hugeness and his voracious appetite. He was followed by a long, lanky individual answering to the name of 'Long Tom' Thomas. Both men were bearded, shabby of clothing, and each wore a gun on the right hip. Without speaking they drew up their horses and without a greeting dismounted.

'And howdy to you, too,' Josh said dryly, rising to his feet. 'Ain't you fellows a long way from the bunkhouse?'

'Come to see you,' grunted Younger. 'Les Parker thinks you're too big fer your britches. He thinks you oughtta be took down a notch or two.'

'He sent you all the way out here to whup Josh?' asked French, scowling.

'Shet up, dummy,' Long Tom spoke up, spitting a mouthful of tobacco juice at French's feet. 'I'll take care of you after Hoss here takes care of him.' He grinned with a snaggle-toothed grimace. French glanced at Josh who was eyeing the couple carefully.

Josh shook his head. 'Nope. You didn't come all this way just to stove me up some,' he said softly, his eyes narrowed and alert. 'You came to do us in, make up some story for the sheriff and have French and me so we can't say anything about what has been happening here on the ranch.'

Hoss glanced at Long Tom, and then swept a meaty hand down to the butt of his gun. He stopped the gesture and grunted, a surprised look on his face. Before his fingers had touched the butt of his gun, Josh's sixgun appeared in his fist, the hammer eared back and pointing at his belly.

'Now you boys drop your gunbelts and back up.' Josh waggled the gunbarrel. 'Now!' he said sharply, and without speaking fired a round into the ground

between the two. Their mounts whirled at the blast
and raced away. Long Tom stared at Josh, his eyes
suddenly wide with fear.

'Parker . . . he . . . he said it'd be a easy thang,' he
stammered, thrusting his hands skyward, trembling.
'He . . . he didn't say anythang about you bein' a
shootist!'

'Never mind what he said or didn't say,' Josh said,
his voice steady and cool. 'Now drop those guns.
French, pick up their pieces and throw them into the
creek.'

'Now you look hyar . . . .' Hoss started to protest.
But the gun in Josh's hand spoke again and at the
blast, the gun and holster on the big man's hip flew
off and onto the ground behind him. Hoss gulped
and staggered back.

Hurriedly, Long Tom released his belt and
stepped back, his face suddenly ashen. 'You hain't
gonna shoot us, jist for threatin' to thump you
around a leetle, are you?' he said, his voice quaver-
ing.

Josh did not answer, but watched them carefully as
French retrieved Long Tom's sidearm and tossed it
into the creek a few yards away.

'Now,' said Josh sofly, holstering his gun. 'Roy,
which one would you like to exercise a little? Hoss or
Long Tom?' Josh held his sixgun in his hand as he
spoke, the barrel pointing between the two men.

Roy eyed Hoss Younger. They were close to the
same height and weight. 'I'll waltz with this 'un,' he
pointed a thumb at Hoss. 'You can even let the other
one in if you wanta.'

'Naw,' said Josh. 'We'll save the dessert until last. I
might even go a few steps with Long Tom.'

Hoss suddenly grinned, his eyes gleaming. He was a saloon fighter. He knew the dirty tricks and he was of the size of the man facing him. He remembered Roy French as fat, drunken and seemingly without much grit. He did not see the toughened hands or the slimmed-down waist of his opponent. 'You jist set this one out,' he said to Long Tom. 'It won't be a long wait.'

With that he launched a huge fist at French's face. Roy ducked, but was somewhat slow, and the blow caught him on the point of the shoulder and he staggered back. With a yell Hoss dived at him, to meet a knee in the chest which brought him up short, straightened and French's right fist caught him on the side of the jaw. He staggered backwards, shaking his head and walking on his heels.

Josh was watching Long Tom carefully. The tall, gangly fellow was watching the fighting and winced as Roy's left fist lashed out and caught Hoss coming in. The big man went down and rolled.

Long Tom suddenly moved around back of French and, snatching a piece of limb from the stack of wood close by, he drew back to crash it into French's kidneys. Josh's gun flamed, roared and the club splintered in Long Tom's grasp, sending slivers of wood flying and some burying themselves in his arms, chest and face. He yelled in pain and fear and fell to his knees, cupping his bleeding face in his hands.

Josh turned his attention toward French and Hoss and was startled to see his big friend rolling in the dust, his face a mass of blood from a blow that had crushed his nose. He was further startled to see Hoss reach for his sixgun. Seizing the weapon, he whirled, leveling it at French, who was clambering shakily to his feet.

Josh, having holstered his weapon, reached for it and was thrown back against the cabin step by the lurching, yelling Long Tom. The club, or another, in his grasp, the gangling man reared back to slam it into Josh's head.

There was a muted THUNG and an arrow pierced Hoss's chest. He staggered back, staring down at the ancient weapon of death thrusting halfway from his chest, the steel-pointed head lodged in his lungs.

At the same time another THUNG and SWISH, and Long Tom straightened and then collapsed upon his face, an arrow penetrating his back and into his heart. The force of the arrow was so great it had pierced entirely through Long Tom's body, with bloody point thrusting out of his chest.

The two men fell, their eyes staring, quivering in death. Josh turned, swiftly drawing his sixgun, cocking it on the way to waist-high level. French rolled over and sat up, his hands groping for his sixgun.

'My friend was in great trouble,' Running Fox said. 'I and my brothers decided you needed help.'

The Indian stood at the corner of the shack, his bow now slung across his shoulder. He leveled an unsmiling gaze at Josh Cabel. 'You are too trusting, my friend. That one,' he gestured with his chin, 'was ready to crush your head.'

Two other braves stood nearby, each with a bow, now slung across their shoulders. They looked at Josh, with only a brief nod. French rose to his feet, staring at the bodies with the arrows through them.

'Who . . . who are these Injuns?' he asked shakily, looking first at one and the other, and then at Josh.

'This is my friend, Robert Running Fox,' he told French, 'and the others are his brothers. I lived with them in their village while recovering from being shot in the head.' He turned to Running Fox. 'That is Roy French, my companion here on the mesa. We work together for the Bar-C Ranch.'

Running Fox nodded to French. 'If you are friend of Josh Cabel, then you are my friend, also.' He turned back to Josh. 'My brothers and I will take care of the two who would have injured you. You need not worry about them.'

Josh Cabel and Roy French arrived at the Bar-C main headquarters at dusk the following afternoon. As they arrived Marshal Harrison and Sheriff Spears were standing on the porch of the main house. Sam Crawford stood in the doorway, his face a mask of consuming anger, mingled with fear. Fear which was an emotion unknown to him. Years had gone by, he was solidly a part of the territory. His Bar-C Ranch was known far and wide as an important part of the economy of the area. He was constantly consulted for his opinions on important issues concerning the state and, in particular, this part of the Colorado territory.

Yet here was a United States Marshal staring at him with cold eyes, along with the sheriff.

'I don't know what you need to talk to me about when it comes to gun-running,' he mouthed raspingly. His heart beat fast in his chest and he felt the feeling of doom poised over him.

He glanced aside as Josh and French rode into the ranch and were turning their horses into the corral. Cabel! he thought. Cabel has talked about what he saw in the pueblos! The color drained from his face. He dropped his head and backed away from the door.

'Come on in,' he said hoarsely, his voice tight wih tension, his mouth suddenly dry with frustration and dread. 'I might as well let you get it off your chest, whatever it is.'

Seventeen

Les Parker was in a quandary. He had sent 'Hoss' Younger and 'Long Tom' Thomas to the mesa with orders to eliminate Josh Cabel, and if necessary, Roy French. It was to be made as though the two had died from unknown causes. There were always bad cases roaming the territory. They frequented lonely camps and killed and robbed, if only for food and a horse or two. The loss of the two on the far, isolated mesa could very well be laid to such an incident.

But here was Josh and French, unsaddling their cayuses, tending to them calmly and unhurriedly, as though nothing at all had happened. Had anything actually happened? he wondered. Maybe Hoss and Long Tom had been the ones waylaid by some roaming back-trail riders before they got to the mesa. Or maybe, Josh and French had won in a shoot-out with the two visitors and had buried them in some coulée or cave where the bodies would never be found.

Parker walked out of the bunkhouse, meeting Josh and French as they approached the building with their bedrolls and tarps.

'I'll just bet you two are comin' in, so you can go to the dance at Colorada City on Saturday,' he said.

'Can't say as I blame you. Gets mighty lonesome-like and I reckon the nights are gettin' somewhat chilly out there on the mesa.'

Josh nodded. 'Right on both counts,' he said. 'The dance sounds mighty inviting and it is getting right brisk come sundown out there.'

'First snow you herd the beefs onto them big meadows close to the cliffs. They'll be more protected there, and the snow don't get as deep.' He eyed both men. They had said nothing about 'Hoss' Younger and 'Long Tom' Thomas.

'By the way,' he said rather casually, 'I sent Hoss and Long Tom out your way a few days ago.' His eyebrows rose in question. 'Did they give you my message?'

Josh shook his head. 'Nope. No message from them. Did they come and talk with you?' Josh asked French.

'Nary a thing,' said Roy. 'Reckon they may have gone on into town first, knowin' the dance was being talked of?'

Parker grimaced. 'With them two, you'd never know.' Before he commented further their attention was caught by the voices of Marshal Harrison and Sheriff Spears, as they came out upon the stoop in front of Crawford's office.

'After I get a little more information, Sam,' the marshal was saying, 'I'd be obliged if you would come in to the sheriff's office. We'll have the situation pretty well in mind by then. There may be others we can bring in to give a clearer picture of what has been happening concerning supposedly illegal gun-running on your property.'

Parker saw Crawford standing in the doorway, his

face stoical, his eyes glinting. Crawford simply nodded when the marshal spoke and, turning his back upon them, entered the house.

Sam Crawford sat in his office pondering what seemed slowly developing toward a catastrophe for him. He had never seen the weapons cache. But he knew it was there, had given permission for the guns to be hidden on his ranch. He had put up money for their purchase, but had nothing to do with the dealings before and afterwards.

Now he was apparently the chief suspect in the deal. And the marshal had told him that an Indian agent, Sanders, who had engineered the deal, was dead. He knew this. He knew who had committed the murder. And that he himself, for the safety of himself and Parker, had ordered it. For Les Parker was, actually, when all was said and done, the main cog in the machine. Yet he could not tell the marshal this, without implicating himself.

His thinking was shattered by the presence of his daughter in the doorway of his office.

'Hi, Daddy,' she said, coming to him smiling. 'I'm going into Colorado City for the dance. Are you coming?'

He eyed her. Where had his little girl gone? Here was a full-blown young woman, beautiful and shapely, vibrant and radiant in her young womanhood. One day some swain would appear at the door asking for her hand and he would . . . he shook his head. She would take that hand in all probability and start her own life without her father.

'No, honey. I ain't goin' to the dance. Have one of the boys or Les Parker side you. Don't go in by yourself and if there's no one to come home with, stay with the Widow Guthrie.'

'Oh, I'm not going by myself, Daddy. Josh Cabel is going with me. He's outside right now with our horses.'

Crawford winced and then managed to smile. 'Well, I guess that does it then. You go an' have a good time, an' dedicate one dance to your old dad, huh?'

She smiled and coming to him leaned over and kissed his cheek, resting her head against his momentarily. 'You've got it, Daddy, the first dance is for you.' Crawford grimaced as she danced from the room. Of all his hands, Josh was the one he would rather she not go with. But . . . what could he say? Don't go with him, for he knows about my gun-running?

She turned in the doorway, smiling, her teeth white against the light tan of her features. She fluttered fingers at him. 'Bye, Daddy. You get some rest. I'll see you tomorrow.'

She almost danced down the steps from the porch to where Josh stood, holding the reins of his horse and the pretty little mare her father had given her when she returned from the Denver 'finishing school' for girls.

She took the reins from him and smiled as he aided her into the saddle. She had been riding since she was three years old. She had leaped into her own saddle, crawled aboard her pony since she was eight. But she demurely gave her hand to Josh and allowed him to assist her mounting the mare. Her face was rosy with her inward thoughts as his strong hands lifted her with ease.

Les Parker came out of the corral where he was inspecting a newly purchased stud, and watched them canter up the lane leading to the main trail into Colorado City. He scowled. Cabel was getting all too friendly with the boss's daughter, he thought. Through the years of Saralou's growing and developing, the foreman had treasured the thought that perhaps, just maybe he and Saralou . . . he shook his head. He was thirty years older, set in his ways. And there was an unsavory period in the past. He sighed and shook his head again, and watched the two younger people disappear around a bend in the trail.

'I'll go down to the Widow Guthrie's and dress. Will you come for me about dusk? The dance will be starting soon after.' They had drawn up at the edge of town after a trip of laughter, stories and long, introspective periods, especially on Josh's part. He was still dazed that this gorgeous young woman, full of laughter and life, had asked *him* to escort her to the dance. He felt awkward and whenever she touched his arm or hand, hot and thrilled within.

'I'll be here,' he told her. He took the reins of her mount. 'I'll take the horses to the livery and get them settled.'

The fiddler was tuning his instrument, the guitars adding to the discordant noise. People were gathering at the dance platform between the Methodist Church and the mercantile. Hitch rails were provided for riders, and the buggies and buckboards were drawn up a few yards down the street. An air of congeniality prevailed, groups gossiping, exchanging information on cattle prices, weather and other issues of momentary interest.

Josh and his pretty escort arrived as the first couples were stepping onto the platform. A little girl, in a fresh gingham dress, was standing at the head of the steps, collecting for a Sunday School project. Coins rattled into her box and her smile brought equal smiles from the contributors.

The musicians were ready and swung into an introductory tune. Couples sepped out onto the floor and moved into a slow waltz. Josh reached and took Saralou's hand.

'We might as well get our evening started,' he said. 'I expect at least half of your dances. I see plenty of young fellows eyeing you. I may have to get a club to keep them away.'

'Don't you dare!' she said, laughing, her teeth flashing. 'You shall have at least every other dance, if not more.' She put her hand upon his shoulder and they swung into the steps, her body close to his and her breath sweet upon his face.

At a time when Josh had relinquished Saralou's hand to another asking for the next dance, he stepped off the platform for a smoke. He was rolling the cigarette from his sack of Bull Durham when Les Parker moved out of a group of men he had been talking with and came over to him.

'Hey, Josh. Enjoying yourself with the boss's daughter?' He chuckled as he spoke, but Josh detected a note of derision in his voice.

'Yeah, Les. Saralou is a great dancer.'

Les leaned against a platform post beside Josh. 'Have you seen Crawford? I guess he is here. I didn't see him when I left the ranch.'

Josh shook his head. 'Nope. Saralou said her dad was not coming. He didn't tell her why not. If he's here, I ain't seen him.'

Les shrugged. 'I guess he's old enough to take care of hisself,' he said. Josh noticed a restlessness about the foreman.

A figure moved from the shadows of a building at the head of the street and approached the dance platform. As Josh recognized Deputy Federal Marshal Harrison, Parker slipped away into the darkness and joined the group with whom he had originally been talking before he came over to Josh.

'Cabel?' The marshal stopped before him and peered in the darkness. Torch flares and a few lanterns provided the only light for the area. 'Good. I wanted to talk with you.'

Josh dropped his cigarette and ground it out with his boot. 'What about, Marshal?'

The lawman was silent a moment, eyeing the crowd about the platform. He sighed. 'I'm gonna have to bring in your boss, Crawford, on this gun-runnin' deal. I'd like you present, also, and your foreman, Parker.'

Josh was puzzled. 'I know why you want to have me present, for I found the cache and told the sheriff about it. But, why Parker? I don't know that he was involved.'

'Maybe not,' the marshal replied. 'But I have a fellow in Denver who saw someone lookin' like Parker, ridin' away from the Sanders house, the night Sanders was murdered!'

A shadowy figure slipped away from the dance platform. No one noticed nor did they hear the soft sounds of a horse leaving the hitch rail in front of the Red Dog Saloon. The rider walked the horse quietly until he was at the edge of town, and then put spurs to the animal.

In a few moments he was gone, the darkness of night and the sounds of the dance covering any noise of his leaving.

Eighteen

Dawn was just pushing back the darkness of the night, spreading fingers of mauve and rose across the heavens. But Les Parker, as he stepped from his horse, saw none of this.

He walked up to the porch of the big house and raised his fist to knock, when it was opened before him. Sam Crawford stood there, his hair tousled, his eyes red with tension and sleeplessness.

'Sam, we've got to talk,' Les said shortly. He pushed past his boss without invitation to enter, and led the way into the untidy office. Sam followed him, his shoulders slumped with fatigue. He had not slept for the last two nights. His mind was awhirl with thoughts of what might happen to him, to his ranch ... to his daughter.

'We do,' he agreed. He dropped with a sigh, into the chair behind the desk. 'And it concerns both of us. We are at the point of being in a mess of trouble.'

Parker did not sit in the chair before the desk. He leaned one shoulder against the wall and stared at Crawford. 'I overheard Josh Cabel talking with that federal marshal. The marshal is going to bring you in

135

to the sheriff's office, along with me and Cabel. He knows I shot that Indian agent in Denver, and if he can't get me for my part of the gun-runnin', he'll nail me for shootin' the agent.'

Sam stared at him, his eyes narrowing. 'I ain't gonna take the fall for you, Parker. You brought the idea of the guns to me. I furnished the money and a place to store them. But I ain't set eyes on the place where they was, nor on any of the guns. You will take the responsibility. An' so far as Sanders is concerned, I just told you to shut him up. I didn't say kill him!'

Parker's face tightened. He pushed off the wall and putting his hands upon the desk, leaned over, his face close to that of the rancher. 'You ordered Sanders' death! I done what you wanted done! Now, I ain't goin' to no prison for life, or to a scaffold for you, or no one else! If this goes down, we go together!'

'Why you . . . .' Crawford half rose from his desk and clawed for a drawer in which he kept a loaded revolver. 'You threaten me . . . .'

Parker was thinking, there was no one on the ranch right then, except a Mexican woman who did the cooking for Crawford and acted as housekeeper, and old 'Cookie' who did the cooking for the hands and served them in the mess shack beside the bunkhouse. But a gunshot would alert at least one or both of them. The rest of the hands who had attended the dance at Colorado City would be in soon. And he knew Saralou and Cabel would be in before noon. So right now . . . .

He launched himself across the desk as the rancher pawed at the drawer containing the handgun. The weapon was of a smaller caliber than the

.44 or .45 usually carried by the ranchers and cowhands on or off the range. Sixguns were as prevalent and considered as necessary as the bandanna in a dust storm.

Parker's fist crashed into Crawford's face, knocking the older man back into the chair. The chair slid with his weight and thumped into the wall. The impact caused Crawford's head to knock against the wall, dazing him. Parker's body slid across the desk and the two men grappled, each attempting to reach a handgun, or slug the other with such force as to knock him aside and gain the advantage in the fight.

The weight of the two range-hardened men was too much for the chair and it broke, tossing them to the floor. Crawford failed to reach the gun in the drawer. Now, he seized a round of the dilapidated chair and swung viciously at Parker's head. Parker saw the blow coming and ducked, taking the blow upon his shoulder. He grunted in pain and threw a knee into Crawford's groin. The rancher screamed in pain and folded, holding himself.

Taking advantage of the moment Parker started to draw his sixgun. But Crawford saw the hand flashing down to the foreman's side and heaving, threw Parker away from him. He rolled and came to his knees, pausing and then rising to a crouched position.

Parker's fingers slipped from the gun and down to his boot-top, to come up holding a skinning knife. The blade gleamed dully in the dimly lit room. Crawford gasped and scrambled back, putting distance between himself and Parker. But the younger man leaped forward, thrusting viciously at Crawford. The knife entered the soft belly just above

the belt and as it did so, Parker twisted it and pulled
upward. The point of the knife sliced into Crawford's
heart.

The rancher looked down at the knife, still held in
Parker's hand and up to the hilt in his body. His eyes
dulled and he looked at the foreman and shook his
head. Blood gushed from his mouth and down over
his chest. His hands, shaking with pain and lost
strength, wavered upward and then he began to fall,
turning aside, and slipping down the wall. He
dropped to the floor and rolled over. His body quivered and he gasped once more, and then relaxed,
caught in the grim fingers of death.

As Crawford fell, the knife slipped from Parker's
hand. Now he leaned over and pulled it from the
body of the rancher. Wiping it on Crawford's pants,
he returned it to the boot sheath. He looked down at
the body of the rancher and grimaced again. He had
not intended it to go this far, but perhaps it was for
the best, he thought.

Going to the desk, he opened the drawer in which
he knew Crawford kept a box with the immediate
cash needed now and then in ranch dealings.
Opening it he removed a large sheaf of bills found
there. A quick count showed at least five hundred
dollars. He thrust the money into his pockets and,
turning, walked to the doorway. He glanced back at
the inert body and then stepped from the office into
the hallway leading to the front of the house. He
paused and listened, hearing no movement in the
house. Apparently the Mexican housekeeper had not
yet arrived. He left the hallway and stepped out upon
the porch. Glancing about he saw no one. He caught
the scent of woodmoke and knew 'Cookie' was up

and stirring the fire in his cookstove for breakfast. Hungry men would be arriving soon after a night of drinking, dancing and carousing in Colorado City.

Mounting his horse he rode quietly out of the area, past the corrals and gigged his mount into a canter. He left the main ranch headquarters and at the end of the road leading into the barns, sheds and corrals, spurred the horse into a lope and headed toward the distant blue rim of the mesa.

Josh Cabel is in town, and will be late bringing Saralou home, he reasoned. He and French will be delayed at the ranch because of Crawford's death. The sheriff and minister will have to be called in from Colorado City. Thus, he further reasoned, he had at least three days, perhaps four, before anyone figured out his part in the killing and started a search for him. There were many places for a man to hide in those old pueblos, beyond the mesa in the canyons and mountains. He held his horse to an easy lope, knowing he had enough time to save the horse's strength, and his own.

Old Gus Brooker, 'Cookie', stepped to the door of the cook shack. He heard hoofbeats, not hurried. This puzzled him, for most of the boys brought their mounts in quickly, the echo of their arrival bouncing off the buildings and invading the cook shack where Cookie spent the majority of his time. He stepped to the door, wiping his hands upon a soiled apron. Parker was just disappearing past the corrals. The old cook watched until he saw the foreman turn toward the far mesa and disappear over a slope in the prairie. He shook his head. Something was up, something wrong, for Parker to be taking off like this, and saying nothing to anyone. Undoubtedly he and Crawford had made some decision that was sending the foreman to the furthest reaches of the ranch.

The first of the cowhands arrived, bleary eyed and somewhat infirm upon their feet. They put the cayuses into the corrals, tossed the equipment into the tack shed and struggled into the cook shack where Cookie handed each a tin cup of steaming black coffee, strong enough to burn away their cobwebs and get their eyes propped open.

They were into their steaks and spuds when there was a wild, weird scream from the direction of the main house. The hand nearest the door quickly stepped out and saw the housekeeper standing in the porch, weeping and wringing her hands, and screaming at the top of her voice.

'Señor Crawford . . . *Oh Dios* there is *mucho* blood!' she screamed as she saw the cowboy emerge from the cook shack. 'Señor Crawford is . . . *muerto* . . . I think!'

The hand turned and yelled into the cook shack. 'Something's wrong up at the house. The Mex woman is screaming about Crawford's blood!'

The cook shack cleared as all the hands dropped their forks and knives and, following the one who had alerted them, raced toward the main house.

The Mexican housekeeper met them at the porch and pointed into the hallway. 'He's in the office . . . *Dios* . . . the blood, everywhere!' she wept, holding her apron over her face.

'Wa'al, why're we standin' here? Let's get in there and see what it's all about,' Cookie took over the direction of the next moves. He entered the hallway and went to the office door. Crowding him were the other men, some craning their necks to see around the cook. The cook saw the body of his boss and, pausing momentarily, entered and knelt beside the body. He placed a hand against the neck and, bending, listened at the nose and mouth. He rose stiffly to his feet, his face grim.

'He's dead, all right. Been stabbed in the belly an' cut bad. Someone shore stuck him.' Several of the others crowded in and then followed Cookie from the room. Cookie turned to one of them.

'Slim,' he ordered one of the men, 'have the Mex woman give you a blanket an' cover him. I guess then we just wait 'til Miss Saralou and Josh show up.' He shook his head. 'Shore will be a sad thing fer her.'

Josh, with the young woman beside him, rode into the corral area and saw the men crowded around the porch. Some were smoking, some were standing watching him and the boss's daughter arriving. Turning his horse, Josh rode up to the hitch rail in front of the porch and dismounted. He had seen the distressed expressions on some faces of the men, others stoical and non-committal. But, with them all gathered here, he was aware that something bad had happened.

Saralou dismounted as he did and approached the men, a smile on her face. When Cookie stepped down to meet her, the smile slowly faded and became an expression of bewilderment.

'What is wrong, Cookie?' she asked. 'Why is everyone here? Where is Daddy?' She swept a quick glance and saw her father was absent.

Cookie shook his head. Josh came up beside her. She felt him there and her heart lurched. Something had happened. She felt comforted that Josh was there to lean on.

'Miss Saralou, I've got some awful bad news, jist awful,' the old man said softly, his hands twisting in the apron which he still wore. 'Someone done kilt yore pa, Miss Saralou. An' no one knows who done it.'

She wilted slightly and wavered for a second. Josh put a hand upon her shoulder and squeezed, his sympathy reaching out to her.

'Why . . . how . . . who would do such a thing?' she stammered, tears beginning to course down her cheeks. 'It must have been a robber. Someone tried to rob him,' she said more firmly. 'And he fought and . . . got terribly wounded. Is that it?'

Cookie nodded, sensing this was the best explanation for the moment. 'That musta been it, Miss Saralou. An' he surely put up a fight, he was a strong man. But he couldn't live after all was done to him.'

'Where is he? I have to see him!'

Cookie nodded. 'We put him on the couch in the sittin' room,' he said. 'But it ain't a purty sight. I . . . I think best you jist rest . . . .'

She pushed by him and into the house. The Mexican housekeeper met her and took Saralou into her arms. She murmured comfortingly and hugged her. Together they went into the living room where the earthly remains of Sam Crawford lay, covered by a blanket.

Josh pulled Cookie aside. 'Have you sent for the sheriff?' he asked.

Cookie shook his head.

'Where is Parker? Isn't he around?'

Cookie shook his head again. 'Nope. Last I see'd of him, he was ridin' out beyond the corrals.' He paused and then added, 'Looked like he was headed toward the mesas.'

Josh thought a moment. 'Send one of the men in for the sheriff and for the minister. I'll go talk with Saralou.' Cookie nodded and walked back to the gathered men on the porch.

They sat on a bench back of the house, beneath a pine beside a small garden which had been planted and was tended by the Mexican woman.

Saralou's tears had ceased. She asked the age-old question of 'why', which to an extent, Josh tried to answer.

When he told her of the hidden cache of guns and explained the possibility that having the guns on the Bar-C Ranch would cast suspicions upon her father and the foreman, she listened quietly and then slowly turned her face toward him. When he finished, she rose slowly and faced him.

As she stepped away from him, her face was white, calm and devoid of expression. 'My father would never let himself become involved in such a scheme,' she said coldly. 'Nor would Les Parker. Why, I've known Les,' her voice broke and tears rolled down her cheeks, 'known him all my life. He put me on my first pony, taught me to ride . . . .' Her voice shook, then she slowly regained her composure. Her eyes narrowed and gleamed as she faced him.

'That you could have done what you did, involving

my father and Les, makes me hate you! Get off this ranch! I never want to see your face again!' She glared at him and, turning, ran weeping into the house.

Nineteen

Les Parker, once out of sight of the ranch headquarters, gigged his horse into a long, mile-eating lope and headed toward the blue rim of the mesa in the far distance.

He knew the sheriff and the federal marshal would see through the murdering of Sam Crawford and immediately initiate a search for him. He reasoned that he would reach the line shack late in the day. Both Cabel and French had come in for the end-of-roundup dance and would not be on the mesa for at least another day.

He would provision himself with what he could find in the shack and then disappear into the canyon and brakes of the mountains. Vaguely, he recalled hearing of an old outlaw trail that led through the mountains from Colorado into the Wyoming territory. Once there he could forget about the law behind him.

He grew grim at the thought of Josh Cabel being the one who brought the law onto him. Sam Crawford, Parker knew, had been only peripherally involved in the deal. He had provided the place for the cache to be left until taken by the gun-runners, and had also bankrolled the deal. He had never seen the guns, nor dealt with those receiving them for trading or sale to the Indians. Les Parker had handled all that.

But, Crawford was part of the deal which would put a hundred repeating rifles, .44-caliber Henry Repeaters, with ammunition, into the hands of Indians sworn to drive the advancing pioneers and soldiers back beyond the Mississippi. As such an accessory he would be equally as guilty as Parker or the agent receiving the guns.

Now, he could not blab all he knew. Parker winced when he thought of Saralou. He loved the young woman as his own daughter. He had taught her to ride, provided ponies and then mares, well gentled for her use. He had seen her develop from a gangling girl, all knees and elbows, to a buxom young woman, whose coming of age and maturity were attracting the attention of young men in the area. He doted upon her, even more than her crusty father. But now she would find out about his and her father's attempt to become rich at the cost of blood and lives, and would undoubtedly cringe for the rest of her life at the thought of them.

The wind was cool upon his face. The mesa was near. He put behind him the thoughts of what had been, and began to plan for the next moves ahead. He was a criminal in the eyes of the law, and would be so for the rest of his days. He pulled the horse up for a rest and rolled a cigarette, lighting it and drawing the smoke deep into his lungs.

Allowing himself rest for an hour, and the horse some graze and a long drink from a small pond,

Parker resumed his ride toward the mesas. It was not far now to the line shack, where he could provision himself and his horse. He would sleep there tonight and tomorrow disappear into the canyons.

Satisfied with his planning he gigged the horse into a long lope and settled into the saddle for the final leg of his trip. The sun was halfway down the sky and would soon seek the peaks of the mountains to the west. He judged he would arrive at the line shack about dark.

High upon a bluff, concealed in the shadow of a large pine, blending into the background of his world, was an observer. He followed the movement of the rider and, judging the direction Parker was headed, would race ahead and conceal himself until the rider was gone by.

Finally, satisfied he knew where Parker was going, he disappeared over the face of a butte, and once above the valley trail the white man rode, he ran tirelessly toward the camp of Robert Running Fox.

Sheriff Mark Spears and Federal Marshal Harrison arrived at the Crawford ranch during the afternoon of the day the rancher's body had been discovered.

In the living room of the spacious ranch home, they gently conveyed their condolences to the daughter and assured her that the murderer of her father would be brought to justice. No mention was made to her concerning her father's past venture with Les Parker in the gun-running violation. The minister had come with them, and he and Saralou, along with Cookie, discussed the funeral. It was to be the following morning. The grave would be beside that of his wife, Saralou's mother, in a small plot at the back of the main house. There shaded by a small copse of aspen, they would lie side by side.

Sitting on the porch after the minister and the others had gone, Saralou and Cookie discussed the future of the ranch. Cookie hesitated and then spoke, rather brusquely to the young woman. 'Josh Cabel has gone after Parker,' he said.

She sat beside him, remaining silent, her face turned away.

'Whatever Josh told you about Parker and yore daddy was true. He didn't know in the beginning just who was involved, but he done right by goin' to the sheriff.'

She turned and with scorn in her voice said, 'He turned my dad in for something he never did!'

Cookie shook his head. 'Nope, Missy, yo're wrong. When he reported the load of weapons and shells to the sheriff, he didn't know fer shore jist who was involved. Jist that them rifles was bein' traded to Injuns, who in turn would murder white folks with 'em. That was all he knew, an' he was right in what he done. That Parker and yore dad was involved is sad. But don't be blamin' young Cabel for doin' somethin' that saved lots of pain, blood and death.'

'You sound like you are on Cabel's side!' she flared at him. 'My daddy will be up there in that grave because Josh Cabel lied about him.'

Cookie shook his head. 'No, Miss Saralou, yo're wrong. In fact, Josh Cabel told the truth, and done a big favor for the white soldiers, ranchers and homesteaders in this area. That yore daddy and Les Parker was involved was bad, real bad. But Josh, if he is the man I think he is, would have gone to yore dad and to Parker and braced them with what he knew and what he was goin' to do. Think it over, Missy. Don't go blamin' someone else for what your daddy and the foreman did.'

Twenty

Josh Cabel left the headquarters of the ranch, follow-ing the trail toward the mesa, the direction Cookie had informed him Parker had taken.

It was not long until he identified the hoofprints of Parker's horse in the trail dust, the length of the stride indicating Parker had his horse on a long, mile- and time-eating lope. He'll be at the line shack by dark, Josh mused. Will he stay there, or will he go on?

Knowing the distance he had to go, and that Parker was a full day ahead of him, Cabel kept his horse at an even pace, conserving both the horse and himself. Having left the ranch in the afternoon, he knew he would make a cold camp and rousing early in the morning, arrive at the line shack about midday.

His thoughts were bitter. He was sorry it had all happened the way it had. Who could have guessed that Parker would kill Sam Crawford? That he himself had brought this sorrow upon Saralou twisted his heart. He was in love with the young woman. Now, all that he had dreamed of happening

150

was lost. He shook his head. Life took sudden turns and no one could really guess when it would happen, or why.

Pausing beside a small creek, he rested in the shade of aspen and oak and allowed his horse to drink. The sun was reaching toward the towering peaks, determining the amount of light for the day. He knew he was several miles from the mesa. But there were still some hours of sunlight and dusk. He could make his camp in the darkness, picket his horse, and wait out the night.

In his blankets, having eaten a cold beef sandwich Cookie had made for him, and drinking long from the small rill that flowed past his camp, he settled in for the hours before him. He wondered where Parker might be, and if he expected someone to follow him? With the thought on his mind he drifted in and out of sleep.

It was nearing noon when Josh reached the creek below the shack, and allowed the horse to drink again. Gigging the horse gently he rode up the slope to the building.

'You look for Parker?' Running Fox stood at one corner of the line shack, his dark face stoical, his black eyes following Josh as the cowboy dismounted and twisted the reins of his horse about the hitch post before the shack.

He was not startled at the presence of the Indian. In fact, he had expected him sooner or later. Nothing moved in this part of the mountains without Running Fox knowing. His scouts were out constantly, feeding information to the village chief, and to Robert Running Fox, his war-chief.

'Yes, I'm looking for Parker,' Josh replied. He squatted on the creek-stone slab that formed the step for the shack, and rolled a cigarette. Drawing in the smoke, he offered the sack of tobacco to the Indian. Running Fox accepted the sack, and rolling his cigarette, squatted beside Josh.

'We know where Parker is camped. You want to go there?'

'Yes,' said Josh. 'I want to go there. Parker killed Sam Crawford. I want to bring Parker in for the law to handle.'

Running Fox nodded. 'Eat, then I will take you to him.'

It was dark in the small canyon where Les Parker had made his hideout for the moment. He was resting, thinking over his options, and planning his route of escape.

Smoke rose from his small fire, lifting in the moist canyon air. Josh smelled it as soon as Running Fox indicated the location of the hideout.

'I will go in alone,' Josh told the Indian. 'This is my problem, not yours.'

Running Fox nodded. 'A man must face his enemy alone. It is what a man must do.' He watched as Josh leaned over and wrapped the leather thong at the end of his holster about his leg and knotted it. Josh straightened and then, nodding to his companion, stepped from the shadows of the boulder where he had hidden to observe the camp.

Parker heard his footsteps from where he was bending to place a trail-blackened coffee pot at the edge of the fire. He placed the pot and straightened slowly, looking across the flames at Josh.

'Somehow I figured it would be you they'd send after me,' he said, with a wry grimace.

Josh shook his head. 'They didn't send me. I came on my own. I wanted to know why you killed Crawford the way you did, and then stole his money?'

Parker shrugged. Josh saw that his sixgun was in the holster. On the left side was a sheathed hunting knife, with an eight inch blade. He had seen Parker throw the knife from twenty feet into the head of a small keg. He had never seen Parker draw his gun, but he suspected he was as adept with the sidearm as he was with the knife.

'I guess it didn't matter who came,' Parker said. 'For I ain't going back to face no law, marshal, sheriff or jury. You'll have to kill me to take me in, and I have notions about that. I ain't an easy kill.'

Josh shook his head. 'I didn't come to kill you, Parker. I came to take you back and let the law take care of you.' Josh sensed the former foreman of the Bar-C ranch was slowly working himself into the moment of drawing his gun. The way he moved, his expression. He remembered what Sam Bass had told him while teaching him how to handle a sixgun. 'Watch the eyes,' he had said. 'Eyes will give away their plans, what they're gonna do a few moments afore they move. Watch their eyes!'

Parker straightened, shrugging his shoulders, settling into a stance, legs slightly apart, his balance evenly divided upon each foot. His expression was cool, his eyes narrowed. His right hand rested against his gunbelt just above the weapon.

'Why did you have to kill Crawford?' Josh asked, easing himself around, turned slightly sideways to Parker. 'He was your partner in the gun deal. With

you out of the picture he might have been able to
talk the law into believing he had little or nothing to
do with it. Why gut him like a fish?'

Parker grimaced. 'He was weak. The minute I was
gone, he'd have been whinin' to the law how I
tricked him into goin' along with him. Besides, he
was reachin' into a drawer where I knowed he kept a
thirty-eight pistol. I just beat him to it, was all. Once
I started, I knowed I had to finish him.'

Josh sighed. 'Well, why don't you just shuck off
your weapons and come on in with me peaceably?
The army has the guns, the agent that planned the
deal is dead. You might be given a light sentence,
spend a few months in jail, and be let go.'

Parker shook his head. 'No. No way, Cabel. Now,
why don't you just walk away and let me disappear?
We'd both be better off.'

'I can't do that, Les. You broke the law and might
have put lives in danger. You played the game and
drew poor cards. It's time to fold your hand and turn
yourself in.'

With a sudden move Parker went for his gun. He
was fast! Faster than Josh, but his speed pulled his
aim and the bullet sliced through Josh's left side,
staggering him backward to sprawl upon the ground.
As he fell, he drew his gun and rolled, pain flaring
through his body as he did so.

The small canyon roared again as Parker advanced
around the fire, and fired the second time, his
mouth twisted in a grimace of anger and determina-
tion. This time the bullet plowed into the ground in
front of Josh's face, just as he released his first round.

Parker staggered back, dropping his sixgun. He
clutched his stomach above the belt buckle, and

stared down at Josh, astonishment on his features.

Pain lancing through his body, Josh rose to his feet, his gun still trained on Parker. Although the man had dropped his sixgun, he still had the knife and was extremely proficient with it. Parker stood swaying, his hands clutching his belly, now covered with blood. He raised his head slowly and stared at Josh, his mouth working.

Then he slumped back and sat down hard, and straightened on the ground. His eyes never left Josh's face. 'You've . . . killed me, Cabel,' he said, coughing as he talked. Blood came out of his mouth and down over his shirt.

'I'm really sorry, Parker,' Josh said, squatting down beside the foreman. 'I didn't want it this way. Yes, you are dying. Is there someone I might contact for you?'

Parker shook his head. 'No . . . no one . . . ' His eyes began to close and then opened to stare fiercely at Josh. 'You've been huntin' . . . fer a man? Man . . . named Baker?'

Weakness was washing over Josh. The first round from Parker's gun had pierced his side and gone through, apparently hitting no vital organs, but the pain and the loss of blood were taking their toll.

'I've been looking for John Baker for two years,' he said. 'But that's not important right now. You have only a few minutes left. Can I do something for you?'

Parker shook his head, then tried to laugh. His voice gargled in his throat. 'You've been workin' . . . for me nearly a year . . . and didn't know . . . .' He paused, his eyes bulged and he coughed, spewing blood. 'I killed . . . Hawkins to keep . . . him from telling you . . . .'

'Telling me what?' asked Josh, wondering what

Parker was getting at, using his final moments of life to tell him something.

'You've . . . been lookin' for Baker . . . an' all the time,' Parker's chest heaved as he struggled for the final words, 'I'm Baker . . . John Baker . . . .' His voice quivered, his eyes rolled back and with a final gasp, he died.

Stunned, Josh Cabel fell back from his squatting position. All this time the man he had sought, with hate and revenge foremost in his mind and life, had been close to him for nearly a year.

Weakness was coming over him. He tried to stand and fell backwards on the ground. His last thought was that Arley Hawkins had tried to tell him the night Hawkins was killed in the saloon. Hawkins's last words had been, 'All the time you've been workin' . . . .'. Scorning him that he had been so close to his goal and had not known that Parker was actually the man he sought.

Blackness was enfolding him when he saw the face of his friend Robert Running Fox. The Indian bent over him and seeing the wound, began stripping his shirt from him.

The last he heard was Running Fox shouting for a companion and then the Indian saying to him, 'Running Fox will help you, not to worry.'

Twenty-One

Josh awakened slowly. He opened his eyes and saw dimly. Gradually his vision cleared and he looked up into the gentle features of an Indian woman. She smiled at him.

'You wake,' she said softly. 'You are in the tepee of Running Fox. You safe and will get well now.'

He looked about and recognized the surroundings. His lips were dry. 'How long have I been here?' he whispered, his voice rasping in his dry throat.

'You have slept four suns,' she told him. 'I am Whispering Dawn, remember? I am sister of Running Fox.'

He nodded. 'I remember,' he said. 'I seem to be making a habit of waking up to see you.'

She smiled again. 'There is someone waiting outside to see you now that you speak,' she said. 'I will get them.'

Josh drowsed again and when he awakened the second time, he looked up into the face of Saralou Crawford. He recalled her words before he left the ranch headquarters, and wondered why she was here. He looked into her face, seeing the sadness there and hurting for her.

She reached out and touched his hand, slowly clasping it in her own, lacing her fingers in his.

'Josh, I am so very sorry for what I said just before you left the ranch. I . . . didn't mean it.' Tears left her eyes and crept down her cheeks. 'I was in shock over Daddy's death, and what it was all about.'

He squeezed her hand. 'It's all right, Saralou. I understand and as soon as I can get about I'll get my gear together and leave. I don't . . . .'

She clung to his hand and shook her head. 'No . . . no, Josh. Sheriff Spears and Cookie explained it all to me. You were right in what you did, and besides, you were not really certain Daddy was involved. No,' she shook her head, 'I don't want you to leave.' She paused and continued, 'You are an honest man and you did what had to be done.'

He looked at her wonderingly, hope suddenly beginning to build in his heart. 'But . . . .'

She shook her head again. 'I don't want you to leave . . . ever.' Her eyes lowered and then looked again into his own. 'I love you, Josh, and if you want me to, I'll go with you wherever you want to go, or stay here . . . I just want to be with you always.'

His hand tightened upon hers. 'That is exactly what I want, too, Saralou,' he said. 'For ever.'